As happy as she was with her life, with the life she'd carved out for herself, she wanted Will.

Maybe it was just lust.

She sighed and then realized that he'd been staring at her.

"Sorry. I guess I'm getting tired. What did you say?"

"I didn't say anything. I was only watching you, regretting that I didn't kiss you when we were on our ride," he said.

Kiss her? "I thought we'd both decided that was a bad idea."

"I like bad ideas," he said.

* * *

Billionaire's Baby Bind
is part of the series
Texas Cattleman's Club: Blackmail—
No secret—or heart—is safe in Royal, Texas…

BILLIONAIRE'S BABY BIND

BY
KATHERINE GARBERA

First Published in Great Britain 2017
By Mills & Boon, an imprint of HarperCollins*Publishers*
1 London Bridge Street, London, SE1 9GF

© 2017 Harlequin Books S.A.

Special thanks and acknowledgement are given to Katherine Garbera
for her contribution to the Texas Cattleman's Club: Blackmail series.

ISBN: 978-0-263-07002-6

Thank you to all of the Mills & Boon Desire authors,
editors and readers who have welcomed me
as part of this wonderful reading family.

One

Amberley Holbrook wasn't too keen on meeting new people; she preferred the company of her horses and keeping an eye on the stables where she worked. Normally her boss, Clay Everett of the Flying E, was happy to let her do what she wanted. But they had a guest on the property who had told Clay that he liked to ride. So as a courtesy Clay had suggested she stop by and introduce herself and offer to take the guest for a ride.

This held little appeal for Amberley. First of all, the dude was from Seattle, and the last time she checked there weren't any real cowboys from there, so that meant he was some kind of city slicker. Second…she and city slickers didn't get along. She would be the first to admit that was all down to her and her lousy attitude, which was something her father had advised her to keep in check if she wanted to keep this job.

Third…well, there wasn't any third. Digging in her heels and refusing to do as Clay had asked certainly wasn't an option. Amberley had packed more into her twenty-four years than most of her peers. She knew she needed to keep her job because she loved the horses she took care of and she certainly didn't want to go back to her family's ranch in Tyler, Texas.

That was something her daddy had been sure to remind her of when she'd called him earlier and told him about Clay's guest. She and her father were close. Her mom had died when Amberley was thirteen and she'd had four younger siblings to watch over. She and her dad had worked as a team to make sure everything on the ranch got done and her younger siblings, ranging in ages from four to ten, were taken care of. Sometimes her dad would say he cheated her out of a childhood, but Amberley never felt that way. She had her horse, Montgomery, and her family, and until she'd turned eighteen, that was all that had mattered.

Amberley understood why she was nervous about this new guest. The city guy had rented a danged Ford Mustang to drive around in this rugged Texas landscape. She could see the sports car parked next to the guest house that Clay had assigned him.

The Flying E was a sprawling ranch built in the heyday of Clay Everett's Professional Bull Riding career. He'd been at the top of his game until a bull named Iron Heart had thrown him. Clay had had a few ups and downs, but landed back on his feet and started a new career as CEO of Everest, a company that provided ironclad cloud infrastructure to companies. Amberley was the first to admit she had no idea what that really was, but it made Clay a nice fortune and enabled him to employ her as his full-time horse master.

She took care of the stables on the Flying E, provided lessons to locals from Royal and the surrounding county and made sure any guest of the Everetts had access to horses. The ranch itself was sprawling, with a large mansion for the main house and several smaller guest houses. Amberley lived in a cottage that suited her to a T. She'd always wanted her own place and lots of ranch land, something that was beyond the budget of a simple barrel racer like herself. So living on the Flying E and working for Clay gave her the best of both worlds.

She took another look at the sports car.

City guy.

As a teen, she'd watched shows like *Gossip Girl* and longed to be in Manhattan, though she'd have stuck out like…well, a sore thumb, but she had liked the fantasy of it.

So perhaps it wasn't quite so surprising that this man was making her curious before she'd even met him.

"Are you going to knock or just stand here all day?" Cara asked as she stood in front of the guest cabin that had been assigned to Will. The cabin itself was really a sprawling three-bedroom cottage that was all natural wood and glass.

Cara was seventeen and also worked on the ranch with Amberley, as her apprentice. She'd brought the teenager with her to meet Clay's new guest to be sure Amberley didn't do anything…well, stupid.

"Yeah. I was just waiting for the music to die down a little."

"I don't think it's going to," Cara said. "I thought he had a baby. You'd think the old dude would put on some headphones."

"You think he's old?"

Cara raised both eyebrows at Amberley. "Most def. He's got a kid, right? So, I'm guessing he must be old—"

"Geez, kid, back in my day we had to boot up a big old DOS machine and wait half a day for our computers to start working."

The voice was deep and rich, like the faux bass line in White Stripes' "Seven Nation Army," and Amberley felt a blush starting at her chest and working up over her cheeks as she turned to look at him. Their eyes met. His were forest green and made her think of the meadow she rode past each morning on her dawn ride on Montgomery.

There was a sardonic note in his voice that she totally got.

He wasn't old.

He wasn't old at all.

He wore a faded MIT T-shirt that clung to his shoulders and lean stomach. He had on a pair of faded jeans that hung low on his hips, and as she glanced down at his feet she noticed he had on Converse sneakers.

He was exactly what she'd been fearing and, if she was honest, secretly hoping he would be.

"You don't look too bad for your age," Amberley said. "I'm Amberley Holbrook, horse master, and this is my apprentice, Cara. Clay asked me to introduce myself and let you know that the stables are available for your use."

"Thanks," he said, holding out his hand to Cara. "Will Brady. Ancient one."

"Geez, dude, I'm sorry. I was just being mouthy. My mom has been warning me about that forever," Cara said.

"It's all right. I probably do seem ancient to a high schooler."

Cara shook his hand. Amberley wiped her hands on the sides of her jeans and took a deep breath and then their hands met. His skin wasn't dry and rough, the way so many of the hands of the men on the ranch were. They were soft, and as she looked down she noticed that his nails were neat and intact, not split from accidentally smashing one with a hammer.

She rubbed her thumb over his knuckles and then realized what she was doing and dropped his hand.

"Anyway... Come over to the stables anytime. I'll have to observe you riding before I can clear you to ride alone."

"No problem. I'll probably stop by this afternoon," he said. "I have a conference call with the sheriff this morning."

"Is this about Maverick?" Cara asked. "I heard you were in town to stop him."

Will shrugged and gave her a self-deprecating smile. "Just going to see what I can find on the internet to track that SOB down."

"I know we will all be glad for that," Amberley said. "I'm pretty much always at the stables, so stop by anytime."

Cara arched one eyebrow at Amberley but kept

her mouth shut, and they turned and walked back toward the stables. She tried to tell herself that he was just a guy…but she knew that he was so much more than that.

Amberley wasn't the kind of woman who had time for gossip or staring at hot guys. Yet she'd found herself riding by his place for the last two mornings hoping for a glimpse of him. Instead she'd had a conversation with Erin Sinclair, Will's nanny, and she'd even cuddled his cute daughter, eleven-month-old Faye.

Will had called down to the stables earlier to say he was going to come by for a ride, but he wasn't sure when the computer program he'd been running would be done. So it could be anytime between now and sunset. She was trying to focus on the work she had to do. There were horses to tame to the saddle, and she liked it that way. She'd always preferred animals over people. They were easy to predict, she thought. She'd grown up in a very large family, and the thought of having her own, well… She liked kids and men, but having to take care of her own brood made her break out in hives.

"You have to admit he's hot," Cara said. "Not old at all."

"He's a city slicker who probably can't tell a horse from steer. Who has time for that?" Amberley asked.

She and Cara were both grooming horses for the newcomers so they'd be able to take a ride around Clay Everett's ranch and get the lay of the land. When Cara had asked Amberley if she could help her out at the ranch, her gut instinct had been to say no. After all, what exactly did she have to teach the high school girl, but Cara had been insistent and one thing had led to another, and now she was in the barn grooming horses with a chatty seventeen-year-old.

"I'm just saying if a guy like that looked at me—"

"Your boyfriend would be jealous," Amberley said. Cara was dating one of the varsity football players.

"Yeah, he would be. For now. Next year he'll be gone and I'll be…I don't know where I'll be. Did you ever wish you'd gone to college?" Cara asked.

Amberley thought about it. At seventeen she'd wanted to get as far away from Texas, her siblings and the ranching life as she could. She'd wanted a chance to be on her own. But her family hadn't had the money for college and, to be honest, Amberley had only been an okay student. No one had been offering her any money for school and this job with Clay had come along at the right time. She'd met his foreman when she'd been rodeoing during her early teens and he'd offered the job.

It hadn't been her dream, but it had meant she'd be out of her dad's house and away from the siblings she'd had to babysit, and that had seemed like a dream.

At times, it was easy to forget she'd once wanted something else from life. She wasn't a whiner and didn't have time to listen to herself think of things that might have been. It was what it was.

"Not really. I have my horses and Clay pretty much lets me have the freedom to run the barn the way I want to. What more could a gal ask for?" Amberley said, hoping that some of her ennui wasn't obvious to Cara.

"I hope I feel like that someday."

"You will. You're seventeen, you're not supposed to have it all figured out," she said.

"I hope so," Cara said. Her phone pinged.

"Go on and chat with your friends. I can finish up the other horse. You know he mentioned he didn't know when he'd be down here."

"Here I am," a masculine voice said. "I hope I'm not interrupting."

Amberley felt the heat on her face and knew she was blushing. She could blame it on her redhead complexion, but she knew it was embarrassment. She could only be glad he hadn't arrived any earlier.

"Not disappointed at all," she said, reaching for her straw cowboy hat before stepping out of the stall and into the main aisle of the barn.

She'd sort of hoped that he wouldn't be as good-looking as she remembered. But that wasn't the case. In fact, his thick blond-brown hair looked even thicker today and his jaw was strong and clean-shaven. His green eyes were intense and she couldn't look away from him.

She told herself her interest in him was just because he was so different than the other men around the ranch.

If he had a pair of Wrangler jeans and some worn ranch boots she wouldn't be interested in him at all. But the fact that he had a Pearl Jam T-shirt on and a pair of faded jeans that clung to all the right spots was the only reason she was even vaguely attracted to him.

She noticed his mouth was moving and she thought she wouldn't mind it moving against hers. But then she realized he was speaking when Cara, who'd come out of her stall as well, looked at her oddly.

"Sorry about that. What did you say?"

"I was just saying that I'm sorry if just showing up messed up your schedule. I do appreciate you being available on my timetable," he said. "If you need more time to get ready I can wait over there."

She shook her head. He was being so reasonable. But she just had a bee in her bonnet when it came to this guy. Well, to all men who came from the city. She wished he wasn't so darn appealing. That maybe his voice would be soft or odd, but of course, he didn't have some silly city voice. Instead, his words were like a deep timbre brushing over her ears and her senses like a warm breeze on a summer's day. Since it was Texas, October wasn't too cool, but it was fall and she missed summer.

But with him... Dammit. She had to stop this.

"I'm ready. Cara, will you show Mr. Brady to his horse?" she asked her apprentice, who was watching her with one of those smirks only a teenager could manage.

"Sure thing, Ms. Holbrook," Cara said sarcastically.

"You can call me Will," he told Cara.

"Ms. Holbrook, can Will call you Amberley?"

That girl. She was pushing Amberley because she knew she could. "Of course."

"Thanks, Amberley," he said.

She told herself that there was nothing special about the way he said her name, but it sent shivers—the good kind—down her spine. She had to nip this attraction in the bud. Will was going to be here for a while helping Max St. Cloud investigate the cyber-bully and blackmailer Maverick, who'd been wreaking havoc on the local residents, particularly the members of the Texas Cattleman's Club, releasing videos and other damning stories on the internet. Will was the CTO of the company, so he was more of a partner to Max than an employee, and rumor had it they were old friends.

"No prob," she said. "How'd you end up here in Royal?" Amberley asked Will while Cara went to get his horse.

"Chelsea Hunt and Max go way back. So she asked for our help to try to find the identity of Maverick."

Maverick had been doing his best to make life hell for the members of the Texas Cattleman's Club. He'd been revealing secrets gleaned from hacking into smartphones and other internet connected devices. He'd made things uncomfortable for everyone in Royal.

"I like Chelsea. She's smart as a whip," Amberley said. And she seemed to really have her stuff together. No shrinking violet, Chelsea was one of the women that Amberley looked up to in Royal. She lived her life on her own terms, and Amberley was pretty sure that if Chelsea liked a guy she didn't have to come up with reasons to avoid him...the way that Amberley herself had been doing.

Cara came back with Will's mount and Amberley went back into the stall and saw her faithful horse, Montgomery, waiting for her. She went to the animal and rested her forehead against the horse's neck. Montgomery curved her head around Amberley's and

she felt a little bit better. She had always been better
with horses than people.

And normally that wouldn't bother her. But it
would be nice not to screw up around men as much
as she just had with Will. She didn't enjoy feeling like
an awkward country bumpkin.

Will hadn't expected to feel so out of place in
Texas. He'd been to Dallas before and thought that
the stereotype of boots, cowboy hats and horses was
something from the past or in the imagination of television producers. But being here on the Flying E had
shown him otherwise.

Amberley was cute and a distraction. Something—
hell, someone—to take his mind off Seattle and all
that he'd left behind there. All that he'd lost. To be
honest, coming out here might have been what he
needed. His baby girl was sleeping with her nanny
watching over her, and he was someplace new.

Max hadn't batted an eye when Will had told him
he needed to bring his daughter and her nanny along
with him to Royal. His friend had known that Will
was a dedicated single dad.

He had work to do, of course, but he'd ridden a
long time ago and thought getting back on a horse
might be the first step to moving on. From his wife's
death.

It was funny, but after Lucy's death everyone had
been comforting and left him to process his grief. But
now that so many months had gone by and he was still
in the same routine, they were starting to talk, and
his mom and Lucy's mom weren't as subtle as they
both liked to think they were, with their encourage-

ment to "live again" and reminders that he still had a long life ahead of him.

Lucy had had a brain hemorrhage a few weeks before she was due. The doctors had kept her alive until she gave birth to Faye. Then they took her off the machines that had been keeping her alive and she'd faded away. He'd asked them to wait a week after Faye's birth because he hadn't wanted his daughter's birthday to also be the day she'd lost her mom.

"You okay?"

"Yeah. Sorry. Just distracted," he said.

"It happens," she said. She spoke with a distinctive Texan drawl. It was so different from Lucy's Northwestern accent that he… Hell, he needed to stop thinking about her. He was getting away for a while, helping out a friend and having a ride to clear his head. He knew he should let that be enough.

"It does. Sorry, I'm really bad company right now. I thought…"

"Hey. You don't have to entertain me. Whenever I'm in a bad place mentally—not saying you are—but when I am, I love to get out of the barn, take Montgomery here for a run. There's no time to think about anything except the terrain and my horse—it clears away the cobwebs in my mind."

He had just noticed how pretty her lips were. A shell-pink color. And when she smiled at him her entire face seemed to light up. "Just what I need. Let's do this."

"Well, before we get started I need to know what your horsemanship level is," she said. "We'll pick our route based on that."

"Summer camp and college polo team," he said.

"I stopped playing about three years ago. I'm a pretty decent rider and keep a horse at a stable near my home. But haven't been riding much since my daughter was born."

"Sounds like you might be a bit rusty but you've got some skills," she said. "I'll start ya out easy and see how it goes."

"I'm yours to command," he said.

"Mine to command? Not sure I've ever had anything with two legs under my command."

He threw his head back and laughed. She was funny, this one. He wasn't sure if she'd meant that to be a come-on, but there was something sort of innocent about her so he guessed not. She was very different from Lucy, his late wife. That twinge he always experienced at the thought of her colored the moment.

"Let's start with a ride," he said.

She nodded. "There's a mounting block over there if you need a leg up. I'll let you go first."

"Thanks," he said, leading his horse to the block and mounting easily. He shifted around in the saddle until he was comfortable. The horse she had him on was easily controlled and led and seemed comfortable with him as a rider.

"So why are you here?" she asked as she mounted her own horse.

He told himself to look away but didn't. Her jeans hugged the curve of her butt and as she climbed on the horse there was something very natural about how she moved. As she put both feet in the stirrups and sat up, he realized she looked more at home on horseback than she had talking to him.

"Ah, I'm here to investigate all the trouble that Maverick is causing. I'm really good at tracking someone's cyber footprint."

She shook her head and then gently brushed her heels against her horse and made a clicking sound. "I don't even know what a cyber footprint is."

He laughed a little at her comment. "Most people don't think about it, but with smartphones and social media apps, we all are leaving a trail that can be followed."

"That makes sense," she said. "You ready for a run or do you just want to take it slow and steady?" she asked as they left the barn area and reached the open plains.

The land stretched out as far as he could see. It was October, so in Seattle it was rainy and growing colder, but the sun was shining down on them today in Texas and the weather was warm. He lifted his face to the sun, taking a deep breath. It was a good day to be alive.

As the thought crossed his mind, he remembered Lucy again and shook his head. He wasn't going to cry for the wife he'd lost or the family that had been broken. Not now and not in front of this strong, sunny cowgirl.

"Run," he said.

"Just the answer I was hoping for. Follow me. I'm going to start slow and then build. This part of the ranch is safe enough for a run."

She took off and he sat there for a moment stuck in the past until she glanced over her shoulder, her long braid flying out to the side, and smiled at him.

"You coming?"

This ride was just the thing he needed to draw him out of the gloom of the past.

"Hell, yes."

Riding had always been Amberley's escape. But with Will riding by her side, she felt more fenced-in than free. Clay had asked everyone at the Flying E to make Will feel welcome and she tried to tell herself that was all she was doing now. He was just another guest, a city boy, at that. He was here temporarily. She didn't like to think about her past or about the guy she'd fallen too hard and too quickly for. But there was something about Will that brought that all up.

Mostly, she realized it was superficial. They were both outsiders to her way of life. But where Sam Pascal had been looking for some sort of Western fantasy, it seemed to her that Will was looking...well, for a cyberbully but also for some sort of escape. There was a sadness that lingered in his eyes and when he thought no one was looking she could see that he was battling with his own demons.

Something she battled herself.

She heard him thundering along behind her and glanced over her shoulder. He sat in the saddle well and moved like he'd been born to ride. It was hard to keep him shoved in the city-slicker box when she saw him on horseback. She turned to face the field in front of them, taking a moment just to be glad for this sunny October day.

It was good to be alive.

The air had the nip of fall to it and the sky was so

big it seemed to stretch forever. She slowed her horse
and waited for Will to catch up to her.

He did in a moment and she glanced over to see a
big smile on his face.

"I needed this."

Two

"Not bad for a city boy," Amberley told him as they allowed their horses to walk and cool down after their run. "I'm sorry I was judgmental about your skills."

Will couldn't help but like his riding guide. She was blunt and honest and it was refreshing. At work everyone treated him like he was the walking wounded and, of course, at home his nanny only discussed Faye. Rightly so. But Amberley didn't. She'd been treating him like a regular guy.

He hadn't realized how much he needed to get away and be with people who didn't know the personal details of his life. There was something freeing about being with Amberley on this sunny October afternoon. He felt for a moment like his old self. Before Lucy.

He felt a pang. Shook his head to shove the feeling from his mind.

"I didn't realize you were judging me," he said.

She tipped her cowboy hat back on her head and turned to gaze at him with a sardonic look. Her face was in shadows beneath the straw cowboy hat, but he could read her body language. She was sassy and funny, this cowgirl.

Distracting.

"I was judging you and it wasn't fair. It's just the last time I was around city folk was when I worked on this dude ranch in Tyler and a lot of them were... well, not very good riders. So I lumped you in with them. I should have known Clay wouldn't have told me to give you free rein if you didn't know what you were doing," she said. She held the reins loosely in one hand, and pushed the brim of her hat back on her forehead with the other.

Her eyes were a deep brown that reminded him of the color of his mocha in the morning. They were pretty and direct and he was almost certain when she was angry they'd show her temper. Will wondered how they'd look when she made love.

Then he shook his head.

This was the first time lust had come on so strongly since Lucy's death. And it took him by surprise.

He shook his head again. "To be fair, I'm not sure he knew my skill level. I think Max asked him to make sure I get the full Texas experience."

"The full Texas? That's funny. Well, this might be about it," she said, gesturing to the pastures.

He skimmed his gaze over the landscape and then settled back in the saddle. It reminded him of some of the places he'd visited growing up. His family had some property in Montana and there was a similar feeling of freedom from the real world here.

"I'm sure riding across the open plain isn't the only thing that's unique to Texas," he said. "You mentioned Tyler—did you just visit that dude ranch?"

"Nah," she said, looking away from him. But before she did he noticed a hint of sadness in her eyes.

"I worked there when I was in high school in the summers. Clay offered me this job after…well, when I was ready to leave my family's ranch. My daddy said I was losing myself by mothering my brothers and sisters and he wanted me to have a chance to have my own life. I'm pretty good with horses. My daddy has a nice-sized ranch in Tyler. What about you? Where are you from? The Northwest, right?"

"Yes. Seattle area. Bellevue, actually. It's a suburb," he said. He'd never wanted to live anywhere else growing up. He loved the mountains and his waterfront property, but after Lucy…well, he'd been struggling to make Bellevue feel like home again.

"I've heard of it. I think Bill Gates lives there."

"We're not neighbors," Will said with a laugh.

She shook her head and laughed. "I'll jot that down. You ready for a ride back or you want to see some more?"

"What's left to see?"

She rocked back in her saddle, shifting to extend her arm. "Out that way is the south pasture—there's a creek that runs through it. Down that way is the—"

"Let me guess—north pasture."

"Ha. I was going to say castration shed. We do that in the spring," she said.

He shook his head. "I'll skip that."

"Guys always say that."

She was teasing him and he observed that her entire countenance had changed. Her relaxed smile made him realize how full and lush her mouth was, and the way she tipped her head to the side, waiting for his response, made him want to do something impulsive.

Like lean over and kiss her.

He slammed the door on that idea and sat back in his saddle to be a little farther away from her. There was just something about her easy smile and the wind stirring around them. And he was on horseback in Texas, so far away from his normal world, that he wanted to pretend he was someone different. A man who wasn't so tired from not sleeping and hoping he was making the right choices all the time.

He knew that nothing would come of kissing Amberley. He wasn't here to hook up. He was here to do a job. Besides that, he wasn't ready for anything else. He knew that. But for a moment, he wished he were.

"Back to the ranch."

She didn't move, but just stared at him—there was a closed expression on her face now. "Sorry, sir, didn't mean to be inappropriate. Follow me. You want to run back or walk?"

"Amberley—"

"I was out of line. I guess I forgot you were a guest for a second."

"Who did you think I was?" he asked.

"Just a guy," she said, turning her horse and making a clicking sound. Then she took off back the way they'd come.

* * *

He galloped after her and reached over to take her reins, drawing both of their rides to a stop.

She took back her reins and gave him a good hard glare. "Don't do that again."

"Well, I couldn't figure out another way to stop you," he yelled. He wasn't sure what he'd stepped into, but he could tell something had changed and he was pretty damn sure he was the cause.

"Why would you want to?" she asked. "I'm pretty sure you want to get back to the ranch and I'm taking you there."

"Don't act that way," he said. "I'm sorry. My life is complicated."

She nodded and then looked away. "Everyone's life is complicated. We're not simple hicks out here on the ranch."

He hadn't meant to hurt or offend her.

And all of a sudden he felt ancient. Not twenty-eight. Not like a new father should feel, but like Methuselah. And he hated that. He'd always been…a different man. His father had said he was lucky and someday his luck would wear thin. But he knew his father wouldn't rejoice in the way his luck had run out. Losing Lucy had changed him, and some people would say not for the better.

"I'm sorry," he said. The words sounded rusty and forced but they weren't. She didn't deserve to be treated the way he'd treated her, because he wanted her and he knew he wasn't going to do anything about it. He wasn't about to invite another person into the chaos that his life was right now.

"What for?"

"That sounded…jerky, didn't it? Like I'm trying to imply that your life isn't complicated," he said. "That's not at all what I meant. I just meant I'm a mess and this ride was nice and you are wonderful…"

He trailed off. What else could he say? He thought she was cute. Maybe he'd like to kiss her, if he wasn't so stuck in that morass of guilt and grief. And then more guilt because his grief was starting to wane. And it's not like Lucy would have expected him to grieve forever, but moving on was like saying goodbye again.

"I wouldn't go that far," she said.

"What?"

"Saying I'm wonderful. I mean, I have faults like everyone else," she said. Her words were light and obviously meant to give him a way back from the dark place he'd wondered into. But in her eyes he saw weariness and he knew that she wasn't as…well, un-damaged as he had believed she was.

"You seem like it from here," he said at last.

"Then I better keep up the illusion."

But now that she'd brought it up he was trying to see what there was to the young horsewoman. She seemed uncomplicated. He thought about how when he was her age, life had been pretty damned sweet.

"Tell me," he prompted.

"Tell you what?" she asked.

"Something that isn't wonderful about you," he said.

"Ah, well, I think that would be easy enough. I have a short temper. I believe I gave you a glimpse of that a moment ago."

"You sure did," he said with a laugh. "But that could also be called spunk. I like feisty women."

"You do?" she asked, then shook her head. "What about you? What's one of your faults?"

"Hell, I'm not even sure where to begin," he said. And he knew that he didn't want to open that can of worms. His life was littered with regrets lately. Only spending time with Faye or sitting in the dark working on the computer tracking down code seemed to get him out of his own head space.

"I'm not as clever as I once believed I was."

She started laughing. "Well, I think that's the same for all of us. Race you back to the barn?"

"Sure, but since I haven't ridden in a while I think I deserve a handicap."

"Really?" she asked. "That is such a load of crap. If I hadn't seen you ride out here I might have fallen for it."

"It was worth a try," he said.

The fall breeze blew, stirring the air, and a strand of her red hair slipped from her braid and brushed against her cheek. He leaned forward in his saddle and gripped the reins to keep from reaching out and touching her.

He'd just shoved a big wedge between them. A smart man would leave it in place. A smart man would remember that Amberley wasn't a woman to mess with and he had never been the kind of man who screwed around with anyone.

But he didn't feel smart.

He felt lonely and like it had been too long since he'd been able to breathe and not catch the faint scent of hospital disinfectant. He wanted to sit here until night fell and then maybe he'd think about heading back to the life he had. He wanted…

Something he wasn't in a position to take.

He knew that.

"Hey, Will?"

He looked up, realizing that she'd been staring at him the entire time.

"Yeah?"

"Don't sweat it. I've got a beef with city dudes and it's clear that you have something with your baby's mama to deal with. You're hot and the way you ride a horse makes me feel things I'd rather not admit to, but that's it. You're on the Flying E to work and as a guest and I'm going to treat you like that. So don't think…"

"What do you feel?" he asked.

Will knew he felt reckless and dangerous and he wasn't going to stop now. He wanted to kiss her. He wanted to pull her off the horse and into his arms and see where that led.

"Like I said, I'm not going there."

He shifted in the saddle and dismounted his horse, dropping the reins on the ground to check that the horse would stay, and it did.

Will walked over to her and stood there next to her horse, looking up at her. He was closer now, and he could see her eyes, and he wasn't sure what he read in her expression. He was going to tell himself it was desire and need. The same things he was feeling, but he was afraid he might be projecting.

"Come on down here," he said. "Just for this afternoon let's pretend we aren't those people. I'm not a guest and you're not a ranch hand. We're just a guy and his girl and we've got this beautiful afternoon to spend together."

* * *

Never in her life had Amberley wanted to get off a horse more. But her gut said no. That this wasn't going to be sweet or uncomplicated. And the last time she'd been sweet-talked by a guy it hadn't ended well. It didn't matter that she was older and wiser now. She didn't feel as if she was either.

Riding hadn't helped to chase away her demons back then, when she'd found herself pregnant and alone at eighteen, and it wasn't helping now. He stood there in his clothes, not fake-cowboy duded up the way some city guys dressed when they came to Texas, and to be fair he looked like he fit in. He wasn't chasing a Wild West fantasy, he was here to do a job.

And her job was to make him feel comfortable.

What could be more comfortable than hanging out together?

Dumb.

Stupid.

His hair was thick and wavy and he wasn't wearing a hat, so she could see the way he'd tousled it when he'd run his fingers through it. She wasn't getting off her horse. She was going to be sensible.

Please, Amberley, be sensible.

But she never had been.

She suspected it was because she'd had to be so responsible so young. She'd always had to take care of her younger brothers and sisters. But that was in Tyler, and she was away from there now, with no one to worry about but herself.

And this was safe. He just wanted to spend the afternoon together.

One afternoon.

Surely even she could manage that without having it go to hell.

She shifted and started to turn to swing her leg over the saddle and dismount, then she saw the smile on his face and the look of relief.

He was unsure.

Just like her.

Except he wasn't like her. He had ties. And she hadn't asked about them earlier. There was so much she didn't know. Where was his baby's mother? That baby was pretty damn young to be living with a nanny and her father. Was there any way this could be just an afternoon?

If it was…then the mom didn't matter… Unless they were still together. That would be—

"Hey, before we do this. Where is your baby's mother? I don't want to pry but you're not still with her, right?" she asked.

He stepped back—stumbled was more like it—and she suddenly wished she'd kept her mouth shut.

There was no denying the way all the color left his face, or how he turned away from her and cursed under his breath.

"No," he said, walking back over to his horse and taking his saddle with much skill and finesse.

"We're not still together. She's dead." He made a clicking sound and took off across the field as if the hounds of hell were chasing him, and Amberley guessed maybe they were.

She stood there, a wave of sadness rolling over her. A part of her had died when she'd miscarried. Seeing Will…had made her realize that they were two sides of the same coin. She had no baby and no family and he had a baby and no wife or mother for the child. He was trying to deal with the loss the same way she had been.

She knew that riding helped at times but she'd never been able to outrun the pain. Those memories and the truth of her life were always waiting when she'd gotten off the horse.

She clicked her mare and followed Will close enough to call out if he took a path that wasn't safe, but he had watched their trail on the way out and he made no mistakes on the way back.

She slowed her own horse to a walk as Will entered the stable area and decided that maybe she should just let him go. Give him some space to dismount and leave before she entered the barn again.

She saw the ring that she'd set up earlier to practice barrel racing and rode over that way. Montgomery and she had been partners for the last year or so. And when the Flying E could spare her she took the horse and went and competed in rodeos.

Three

Will had just spent the last ten minutes in the barn trying to avoid a confrontation with Amberley—the woman he'd practically run away from. But he had no doubt she would be avoiding him after his foolish reaction to her harmless question about Faye's mother.

It was hard to think that at twenty-eight he was turning into his father, but it seemed that way more and more. And it wasn't Faye who was forcing the change. It was him. It was as if he'd lost that spark that had always driven him. And the therapist he'd seen for two sessions at his mom's insistence had said that grief took time.

But as he left the barn and spotted Amberley exercising her horse in the ring, he felt that stirring again.

It was lust, because even though he was grieving he wasn't dead, and the feeling was laced with something more. Something much more. She was one with the horse as she raced around the barrels, her braid flying out behind her as she leaned into the curves and got low over the horse's neck, whispering encouragement, he imagined.

He watched her and wanted her.

She stopped at the end of her run and looked over toward the barn. Their eyes met and he felt stupid just standing there.

He clapped.

But that felt dumb, too.

It seemed that he'd left his smarts behind in Seattle, he thought. Everything was different here. He tried to justify his feelings—like he needed an excuse to find a woman pretty or be turned on by her. Yet in a way he felt he did.

But that was his issue, not Amberley's. And it wasn't fair to her to bring her into the swirling whirlpool that his emotions were at this moment.

She nodded and then turned away from him.

Dismissing him.

He'd had his chance and he'd ruined it.

Maybe it was for the best. He had Faye to take care of and a criminal to catch. In fact, he needed to get back to work. Without another glance at her he turned and walked to the golf cart that had been allocated for his use during his stay on the Flying E. He put it in gear and drove to the house that Clay Everett had been generous enough to provide. To be honest, he knew that Clay had a stake in Will finding Maverick, as did most of Royal.

He shifted gears as he drove farther and farther away from the barn and the cowgirl that he'd left there, but a part of his mind was still fantasizing about the way his afternoon could have gone.

His nanny, Erin Sinclair, was waiting for him at the door when he got back.

"Faye's asleep and I need to run to town to pick up some more baby food and formula. Are you okay if I go now?" she asked.

He had hired Erin to help with the baby even before Lucy's untimely death. His late wife had been a product rep for a large pharmaceutical company and traveled a lot for work. Though Will spent a lot of time in his home office, he tended to have a single-minded focus, so he knew that by the time Faye was born, both he and Lucy would have needed help with the baby.

"Yes, go," he said.

He went into the bedroom they used as a nursery and looked down at Faye's sleeping face. He tried to see Lucy in her features but he was starting to forget what she looked like. Of course he had pictures of her but he was starting to lose that feeling of what she'd looked like as she smiled at him. The different feeling she'd stirred in him with one of her expressions that a mere photo couldn't capture.

Dammit.

He turned away from the crib and walked out of the room. He had a monitor app on his phone and had a window that he could keep open on one of the many monitors in his office so he could keep an eye on her.

He walked into the darkened large bedroom that he'd turned into his office for the duration of his stay in Royal. He had four large computer monitors that were hooked up to different hard drives and were all running multiple programs that would determine where Maverick was basing himself online.

Almost all of the attacks had been cyber-based, so Chelsea was working on the theory that he was very internet savvy. In a way that worked in their favor because there weren't many top computer experts in Royal. But then hackers wouldn't be known to many.

One of Will's skills was the ability to look at code and see a digital fingerprint in it. Maverick had habits just like everyone and Will was searching for those, looking for a trail back to the creep's identity.

He opened his laptop after he checked the progress on the different computers and made sure all of his scripts were still running.

He launched his internet browser and searched for information on Amberley Holbrook. He wasn't surprised to see her listed in a bunch of small-town rodeos, stretching from Texas to Oklahoma to Arkansas, as a winner or a top-three finisher in barrel-racing competitions. There was a photo of her winning run in a recent event and he clicked to open it larger in his photo application so he could zoom in on her face. There was concentration but also the biggest damn grin he'd ever seen.

That girl was happiest on the back of a horse.

Why?

He noticed how she was when she was off her horse. On her guard and waiting to see how everyone around her reacted. Given that he was starting to behave that way, he wondered what had happened to force her to build those kinds of walls. She definitely had them.

Why?

And why the hell did he care?

Because she intrigued him. She was different. Funny, sexy, sassy. She made him think of things he hadn't in a really long time.

And he'd just walked away from her. He'd decided he had too much baggage to dally with a woman who was tied to Texas and this ranch. He wasn't here for longer than it took to find the cyber coward Maverick, then he was out of here. And back in the Pacific Northwest, where he could slowly rot from guilt and grief.

That sounded damn pitiful. He had never been that kind of man and he wasn't too sure that Faye was going to want a father who was like that.

He knew he had to move on.

Will had come here in part because Max had asked and also because he knew he had to get away from the memories, get away from the guilt and the grief. But he was in no position to move on. He had to keep moving forward until he figured out what he wanted next. Amberley had been a distraction but also something more. She was honest and forthright. He liked that.

He liked her.

If he were in a different place in his life then the zing of attraction that had arced between them...well, he would feel better about acting on it.

But he wasn't.

And that wasn't fair to her.

Who said life was fair... The words of his therapist drifted through his mind. He'd been lamenting the fact that Faye would never know Lucy and that it wasn't fair.

Well, life might not be, but he knew he couldn't just use Amberley for himself and then leave. That wasn't right.

And he hadn't changed at his core.

But she intrigued him…

Amberley blasted My Chemical Romance as she got ready to go out. It was Friday night and two days had passed since…whatever the hell that had been with Will. She tried to remind herself he was a city dude and she should have known better than to be attracted to him, but that hadn't kept him out of her dreams for the last two nights.

So when her cousin from Midland had called and said she'd be driving through Royal on Friday and did Amberley want to go out, she'd said yes. Normally she was all for comfy jammies and binge-watching one of her favorite TV shows on Netflix, but tonight she needed to get out of her own head.

She was ready to dance to some rowdy country music, drink too much tequila and flirt with some small-town boys who wouldn't walk away from her without a word. It had been a long time since she had blown off steam and it was the weekend. Even though she sometimes acted like she was ready for the retirement home, she was still young.

But she didn't feel it.

There was a weight in her heart that made her feel older than her years. And when Will had said his life was complicated she'd…well, she'd ached because she knew complicated.

She knew what it was like to be a big, fat, red-hot mess masquerading as normal. She'd done that for a year after she'd lost the baby and then gotten the devastating news that she'd never be able to have a child. A part of her should have rejoiced that he'd only seen what she had wanted him to—a cowgirl who was damn good with horses.

But that connection she'd felt with him had made her want him to see more.

And he hadn't.

He hadn't.

She was wearing her good jeans—a dark wash that fit like a second skin—and a pair of hand-tooled boots that her brothers and sisters had given her for Christmas. They had a fancy design featuring turquoise and she'd completed her outfit with a flirty peasant top. She'd taken the time to blow-dry her hair and not just pull it back in a braid, so it fell around her shoulders.

She finished her makeup and put a dash of lip gloss on before grabbing her purse and heading out. She was halfway to her truck when she realized someone was in her yard. Not that it was really her yard, since Clay owned all the property, but that little area in front of her place.

Amberley glanced over and realized the someone was a dog. A ragged stray that was making mewling sounds that she couldn't ignore. He was a rather sad-looking animal with a matted coat. She tossed her purse on the hood of her truck and turned toward the dog, careful not to spook it as she walked toward it. She crouched low and held out her hand for it to sniff once she was close enough.

The animal whimpered and then slowly moved closer to her. She held her ground, noticing that it limped. One of his legs was injured. Just the distraction she needed. Animals were the one thing on this planet that she was actually good with.

She waited until the dog came closer and noticed that there were some briars wrapped around his hind leg, and when she reached for the leg he moaned and moved away from her.

"All right, boy. I'll let it be. But we are going to have to take you to get that looked at," she said. She stood up, pulled her phone from her back pocket and texted her cousin that she'd be a little late. Then she went back into her place, got a blanket, a bowl and bottle of water. Then she grabbed a carrot from the fridge and went back outside.

The dog was exactly where she'd left him. Waiting for her.

"Good boy. You're a boy, right?" she asked.

The dog didn't answer—not that she expected him to. She put the bowl down in front of him and gave him some water and stood to watch him as he drank, then texted the small animal vet that Clay used to let him know she'd be bringing in an injured dog. Though it was after hours, Clay had an agreement for the ranch that included 24/7 coverage.

She spent the next hour getting the dog settled at the vet. He had a chip and the vet contacted his owners, who were very glad to find him. Amberley waited until they arrived before leaving to meet her cousin. But the truth was she no longer wanted to go out.

The dog—Barney—reminded her of how alone she was. Even the stray had someone to go home to. His owners had been really nice and so happy she'd found him and Amberley was gracious to them, but a part of her had wanted the stray to be a loner. To maybe need her.

She hated that she was feeling down about her life. She'd finally gotten past everything that had happened when she was eighteen and now some dude was making her question her situation. She'd never been this knocked on her butt for some guy. Yet there was something about him that had made her want to be more. Want to be someone she hadn't thought about being in a long time.

But there it was.

She wanted to see him again.

Her cousin was waiting in the parking lot of the Wild Boar, a roadhouse that served food and drinks and had a small dance floor with live music on the weekends. There were pool tables in the back and a mechanical bull. If you weren't in the upper echelon of Royal and weren't a member of the Texas Cattleman's Club, then this was the place to hang out.

"Hey, girl. You ready to blow off some steam?"

She nodded. Maybe a night out with Royal's rowdy crowd was what she needed to remind her of where she belonged and whom she belonged with...and it wasn't a hot guy from Seattle.

Midnight was his favorite time of night and when he found the most clarity when he was working—tonight wasn't any different. Faye was a little night owl like he was, so the baby was playing on the floor at his feet while he watched the scripts that were running and tracking down Maverick on the monitor nearest to him.

She'd woken up crying. Erin was worn out from

a long day of dealing with Faye teething, and since Will was up at night working anyway, they'd established that he would take the night shift.

Maverick wasn't the cleverest hacker, but whoever he was, the man was running his internet through a few connections. It would have fooled someone who didn't have Will's experience, but he'd been a pirate hunter in high school for a large software company that his dad had helped found and he'd spent a lot of years learning how to follow and find people who didn't want to be found.

"Dada."

"Yes?" He looked down at Faye. Her face was so sweet and she was holding a large round plastic toy up to him.

He took it from her.

She immediately reached for one a size smaller and held it up to him. This was one of her favorite new games. She gave him all the toys around her and then he had to sit still while she took them back and put them in a seemingly random order in front of him.

But this time she was done handing them all to him, so she crawled over to where he sat on the floor next to her and crawled onto his lap. He scooped her up and hugged her close.

His heart was so full when he held his daughter. She smelled of baby powder and sweetness. He knew sweetness wasn't a scent, but when he held Faye it was what he always felt.

He stood up and walked around the house with her while she babbled at him. He set a notification on the computers to alert his phone when the scripts were finished running and then put Faye's jacket on her so they could go for a walk. He'd grown up in Bellevue, near the water, and some of his earliest memories were of being outside with his mom at night looking at the sky.

He knew that many people would expect Faye to be in bed at midnight, but she wasn't looking sleepy at all. It was probably his fault for having a long nap with her in the afternoon. He'd been keeping odd hours since they had arrived in Royal.

He walked toward the barn, telling Faye the stories his mom had told him. Will's mom's people had been sailors and the sky and the water were a big part of their history.

He heard the rumble of a truck engine and turned as a large pickup rounded the corner. He stepped off the dirt track to make sure he wasn't in the path of the vehicle.

The truck slowed and the passenger-side window rolled down. He walked over and was pretty sure it was Clay Everett. But Will knew if he had a woman like Sophie waiting for him at home, he'd have a better way to spend his night than patrolling his ranch.

"Hey, Will. You okay?" Amberley asked.

He was surprised to see her. She had obviously been out, as she smelled faintly of smoke. Her hair was thick and fell around her shoulders. The tousled tresses, so different from her neat braid, made his fingers tingle with the need to touch her hair.

He regretted leaving her the other afternoon. One kiss. Would that have been so bad? Even Lucy wouldn't begrudge him that. But he hadn't taken it.

So instead a need was growing in him fast and large. Each day it seemed to expand and he knew he was losing control.

"Yeah. Faye's a night owl like me so I thought I'd take her for a walk."

Faye heard her name and started babbling again.

"Want some company?" Amberley asked.

"Sure," he said.

She turned off the engine of her truck and climbed out, coming around by him. Her perfume hit him then—it was sweet like spring flowers. There was a slight breeze tonight and Amberley tipped her head back and looked up at the sky.

"When I was little, my dad told us that if we were really good we'd see a special angel in the sky."

"Did you ever see one?"

"Yeah," Amberley said. She stretched out her arm and pointed to Venus. "There she is."

"That's Venus."

"Show some imagination, Brady. That's my special angel. She watches over me at night."

"Does she?"

Amberley nodded. But she wasn't looking up anymore—she was staring at Faye. "She'll watch over you, too, little lady."

Faye answered with one of her babbles. And Amberley listened until Faye was done and then she nodded. "I know. It's hard to believe that someone up there is looking out for you, but she is."

Faye babbled some more.

"Your mama?" Amberley asked when she was done.

Faye babbled and then ended with "Mamamam."

"Mine, too. They are probably friends," Amberley said.

Faye shifted toward Amberley and Amberley looked over at him for permission before reaching for the baby. Will let Faye go to Amberley and watched the two of them talking to each other. She was good with the baby. He was surprised that Faye had wanted to go to her. She was usually pretty shy with strangers.

He noticed that both of the girls were looking at him.

"She's usually not so eager to go to strangers."

"Well, we're not strangers," Amberley said. "We chatted up a storm while you were holding her."

"You sure did," Will said.

Something shifted and settled inside of him. It was a tightness he wasn't even aware of until that moment. And then he realized that he wanted Faye to like Amberley because it didn't matter how guilty he may feel afterward, he wanted to get to know her better.

Four

The night sky was clear, filled with stars and the waning moon. Amberley tipped her head back, feeling the emotions of the week fall away. The baby in her arms was sweet and soft. She had been cooing and pointing to things as they walked and Amberley fought against the pain in her heart she'd thought she'd finally gotten over.

She loved babies. Loved their smiles and their laughter. The way that they communicated if you just took the time to listen to them.

Her dad had told her that she shouldn't give up on a family, but the hysterectomy she'd had at eighteen had pretty much put paid to that. She couldn't have a baby of her own. So she tended to spoil any kiddos she met.

"You're awfully quiet over there," she said, realizing that Will hadn't said much in the last few minutes. She'd suggested they lie in the bed of her pickup truck and watch the night sky. Will had agreed but only, he'd said, until Faye got sleepy.

"Just trying to get this app to work," he said.

He'd mentioned having an app that could show meteor and comet activity in the night sky and was trying to get it to work. Amberley had spread a blanket she kept for picnics on the bed of the truck and she and Faye had been playing together while he tried.

"If it doesn't work we can just make up stories," she said.

"Like what?" he asked.

"That star over there is Lucky."

"As in it brings luck?" he asked.

"No, its name is Lucky. Sometimes the star falls to earth and takes on the persona of a rock superstar during the day, and at dusk it's drawn back up into the night sky, where she stays steady and true so that little cowgirls and cowboys who are out late on the range can find their way home," Amberley said.

She'd been a huge Britney Spears fan when she'd been about ten and her dad had made up that story about one of the pop star's songs.

"Okay, let me give it a try," Will said. He shifted his shoulders and leaned back against the cab of her truck. Faye crawled over to him and he lifted her onto his lap. The baby shifted around and settled with her back against his chest.

They were so cute together, Amberley thought. She ached for little Faye because even though she had her daddy's love and attention, Amberley knew that one day Faye was going to need her momma.

She just felt close to them because she saw herself in the two of them.

"See that constellation?" he asked, pointing to Sirius.

"Yes."

"That's Lobo and he is really good at catching the people who skunk around in the shadows. Every night he looks down on the earth for clues and then during the day he turns into computer code and helps track down the bad guys."

She smiled. "Like you."

"Yeah. Like me."

"How's that going? Is it okay to ask?"

Faye turned in his arms and he rubbed his hand over her back. He lifted her higher on his chest and she settled into the crook of his neck.

"It's going pretty well," he said, his voice pitched low so as not to disturb his daughter.

"I'm glad. Will you be here for long?" she asked.

"Probably a month."

A month…not enough time for anything serious.

"I'd love to know more about what you do," she said. Sometime between the dancing and talking with her cousin tonight she'd realized that no cowboy or Royal guy could make her stop thinking about Will. Probably not her wisest idea, but she had decided she wasn't going to just walk away unless he pushed her to.

"Stop by anytime and I'll show you. It sounds more exciting than it is. Usually it's me in a dark room with my computers running programs or tracking scripts."

"That is so foreign to me. I spend all my time outside and with animals. I mean, I have my phone, which keeps me connected, but I don't even own a computer."

"I don't see why you should need one," Will said. "Smartphones can do just about everything you'd need a computer for."

"Want me to drive you guys back home?" she asked.

"I don't have a car seat so we probably shouldn't," he said.

She felt silly because she'd been used to riding in the back of the truck from the time she'd been a child. She guessed it wasn't that safe, but there wasn't much out here to cause an accident. It underscored to her the many ways they were different.

But he was only here for a month.

Why was she trying to make it acceptable to get involved with him?

She knew why.

She was lonely. It had been a year since her last boyfriend and she was using that term loosely. She and Pete had hooked up at a rodeo and then gone their separate ways. But she felt something stirring inside of her.

Maybe it was just lust.

She sighed and then realized that he'd been staring at her.

Crap.

"Sorry. I guess I'm getting tired. What did you say?"

He shook his head and shifted around, setting Faye on the blanket next to him. The little girl curled onto her side and cooed contentedly as she drifted to sleep.

"I didn't say anything. I was only watching you,

regretting that I didn't kiss you when we were on our ride," he said.

Kiss her.

"Uh…"

Great. He'd rendered her speechless.

No. He hadn't. She wouldn't let him.

"I thought we both decided that was a bad idea."

"I like bad ideas," he said, leaning in closer. He wasn't touching her at all, but he'd tipped his head and she knew he was going to kiss her.

She licked her lips, tilted her head to the side and met him halfway. His lips were firm but soft and he tasted…good. There was something right in the way he tasted as his tongue brushed over hers. She closed her eyes and forgot about everything except this moment.

Will had tried avoiding kissing her, but with the certainty that the moon would rise every night, he knew he really couldn't keep from falling for Amberley. Tonight, sitting in the back of her pickup truck with Faye, had been one of the first times he'd been able to just enjoy being with his daughter and not think of all she'd lost.

He hadn't felt that gnawing guilt-and-grief combination. And now, when his lips met Amberley's, he'd stopped thinking altogether.

God, he'd needed this.

Just to feel and not think of anything but the way her lips had softened under his.

He lifted his head and looked down at her. By the light of the moon he could tell that her lips were wet from their kiss and her eyes were heavy-lidded. She lifted her hand and rubbed her finger over her mouth.

"Damn. I wish you didn't kiss like that," she said.

Surprised, he tilted his head to the side.

She shrugged. "Just would have been easier to write you off as a city slicker if you didn't know what you were doing."

He threw his head back and laughed at that statement. "Glad to know I didn't disappoint."

Faye stirred at the sound of his laughter and he realized it was getting late, even for two night owls.

"You didn't disappoint... Did I?"

The woman who'd fiercely ridden her horse around the barrels and who walked with a confidence that made him think she could conquer mountains was asking him if he liked her kiss. He patted Faye on the back and she settled down before he looked back over at Amberley.

Her hair was tousled, her lips swollen from his kiss, and he knew that later tonight, when he was alone in his bed, he was probably going to fantasize about doing much more with her.

"You were fantastic," he said. "If we were alone one kiss wouldn't be enough."

She nodded.

"For me, either."

"Good," he said. "Now I hate to do this but I really should be getting Faye back home. But maybe I can see you tomorrow?"

She nibbled her lower lip and he moaned.

"What?" she asked.

"You are making it damn hard for me to resist kissing you again," he said, but Faye had begun to wake up. He needed to get her back and into her comfortable crib.

"Sorry. It's just I like the taste of you."

He groaned.

"I could do with a little less honesty from you, cowgirl," he said.

"I'm not made that way," she admitted.

"I'm glad. I'll see you tomorrow afternoon."

"Okay. I'm giving a riding lesson from one until three, so after that, okay?"

"Perfect," he said. He leaned over and stole a quick kiss because he liked the way she tasted, too, and then he stood up with Faye in his arms and hopped down from the bed of the truck. He glanced back over his shoulder and noticed that Amberley had moved to the tailgate and sat there watching him walk away. It was pretty dark, but he was using the flashlight on his phone. And the moon was full, a big harvest moon that lit up the land around them.

He waved at her and she waved back.

"Good night, Will," she said, and there was a smile in her voice.

"'Night," he returned and then cuddled his daughter closer as he walked back to the guest house.

He kept the image of Amberley watching him walk away until he entered the house and saw the photo of Lucy on the hall table.

He took Faye to her room. He removed her coat and then changed her diaper before laying her in the bed. He turned on the mobile that Lucy had picked out for her and that guilt that he'd thought he'd shaken free of was back.

When Will first came to the guest house on the

Flying E, he'd asked if Clay would allow him to set up Faye's room as it had been in Seattle. He wanted her to feel at home and little things like the mobile and her crib and her toys were important. Clay hadn't minded at all and told Will to make the guest house into his home, which he had. And Erin had been instrumental in making sure everything was set up the way they liked it.

Lucy had been so excited when she'd seen it in a magazine. It was a version of the cow jumping over the moon, similar to one that Lucy remembered from her own childhood. They'd had to search all over to find it. Will had scoured the internet—exhausting every avenue—to find it. He remembered how thrilled Lucy had been when she'd opened the package.

He touched the cow as it spun and instead of thinking of Lucy he remembered Amberley and the way she'd played with Faye while he'd been on his phone trying to get technology to work in the middle of the night.

She hadn't gotten impatient with him the way the nanny sometimes did. He liked how easily Amberley got along with his daughter, but a part of him also knew that Lucy should have been the one holding her daughter.

But she was gone.

This job out here in Texas was supposed to give him perspective and help him finally realize that Faye needed him. It was easier here in Texas to shake off the gloom of the last year. And he was moving forward. Slowly. He hadn't realized how isolated he'd let himself become. His world had shrunk to just his work, and then Faye and Erin.

It had been a while since he'd just had a normal conversation. He and Erin mainly just talked about the baby and her eating habits or how teething was going.

He'd never felt like he would be raising his daughter alone.

He had no idea how to do it.

As much as he enjoyed being with Amberley, she wasn't his forever woman. Will had had that. Faye drifted off to sleep and Will went to his own room to shower away the scent of Amberley and then he brushed his teeth and used mouthwash to try to forget the way her kiss had tasted.

But he remembered.

And he still wanted her. His arms felt empty through the night and when he dreamed he was making love to a woman and he looked at her face, it was Amberley's and not Lucy's.

And the dream left him wide-awake, tortured with lust and need and the kind of guilt that felt like he was never going to be normal again.

When Will had been a no-show for their afternoon ride, Amberley chalked it up to him needing to do his job. Clay had told her that Maverick had struck again. Clay had even been a victim of Maverick. The hacker had made it seem as if Everest's cloud encryption software had been compromised, causing clients to panic. But luckily that had all been cleared up.

So Will was probably deep into his investigation. At least that's what she told herself.

Except he hadn't come around the next day, or the day after. A week later she was beginning to believe he might be more like Sam, the guy she'd hooked up with nearly six years ago, than she'd wanted to believe.

Amberley finally went by Will's place one afternoon only to be met at the door by Erin, holding Faye on her hip.

"Hi, there, Amberley," Will's nanny said.

"Hey. Sorry to bother you. I was stopping by to see if Will wanted to go for a ride," she said.

Erin stepped out onto the porch. "He's not here. He had to go into town to meet with Max and Chelsea. Something about Maverick."

"Clay told me he might have struck again," Amberley said. "I've never really had much patience for bullies. Especially ones like Maverick. If I have beef with someone I take it to them. I don't attack from a hiding place in the bushes, you know?"

Erin laughed. "I do know."

Erin's phone beeped. "That's my timer. I was making some teething biscuits for little Miss Faye here. Want to come in and chat? It's kind of lonely out here."

"It is. I'm used to it, though," Amberley said as she stood up. She glanced at her watch, that old battered Timex she'd been wearing for as long as she could remember. "I could stay for about thirty minutes."

"Good. Come on in," Erin said.

As soon as they stepped into the kitchen, Erin put Faye in her bouncy chair on the counter and went to the oven to check on her biscuits. Amberley went over to play with the baby, who was making her nonsensical sounds again.

She looked into the little girl's eyes and wondered what had happened to her mother. Without really thinking about what she was doing, she turned to Erin, who was putting the biscuits on a wire rack.

"What happened to Will's wife?" she asked.

Erin finished moving all the biscuits to the rack before she took off her pot holder and turned to face Amberley. "She had a brain hemorrhage before Faye was born. They kept her alive until about a week after Faye was delivered. It was heartbreaking."

"I can imagine. Is that when he hired you?" she asked.

"No. Lucy was planning to go back to work so I'd already been hired. They wanted the baby to be familiar with the nanny so the thought was Lucy, Will and I would all be in place from the moment Faye was born," Erin said.

That just broke her heart a little bit more. It sounded like Lucy had been ready for motherhood. That their family was getting settled and then bam, the unexpected. Her daddy had always said that change was inevitable, but Amberley thought it would be nice once in a while if things just stayed on course. Like they should have for Faye's family.

Erin offered her a glass of iced tea. She accepted and stayed to chat with her about the Fall Festival, but she felt uncomfortable in the house now that she knew a little bit more about Will's wife. Lucy. She had a name now, and when Amberley left a few minutes later, she saw the photo on the hall table. Lucy had been beautiful.

It was the kind of classic beauty that Amberley, with her tomboyish looks, could never pull off. She wasn't down on herself; it was simply that Lucy was really different from her. And Amberley wondered if she'd been fooling herself to think the man she'd sat under the stars with could see her as anything other than a distraction from his real life.

She wasn't sure she could see herself as anything other than that.

Determined to remember what she was good at and how great her life was, she spent the next few days with the horses and deliberately tried to shove Will Brady out of her mind.

The following weekend, Amberley went into town for the Fall Festival at the Royal elementary school. It was way past time for her to start decorating for the season. She pulled into the parking lot at the elementary school and realized the mistake she'd made.

There were families everywhere. Why wouldn't there be? This was a family event. Perfect for a Saturday.

She'd come after she'd finished her morning routine with the horses and now she wished she'd stayed on the Flying E with her animals. Instead she was watching everything that she would never have and she hated that.

She'd been devastated when she'd had the hysterectomy. But as her father had pointed out in his sanguine way it was better than the alternative, which in her case would have been death.

But she'd never expected to feel this alone.

She'd always thought when she'd been growing up that she'd one day have a family of her own. And holding Faye a week ago had just reminded her of all that she was missing.

She was twenty-four—too young to feel like this.

She got out of the truck because she felt silly just sitting there. She needed pumpkins. Some to carve, some for making pies and muffins, and some just to use as decorations that she'd keep out until Thanksgiving.

She walked through the playground, which had been turned into the Fall Festival, and tried to make a beeline to the pumpkin patch, but Cara was working at the caramel-apple booth and waved her over.

"Hey, Amberley! I'm glad you showed up."

"You know I need a pumpkin," Amberley said. The booth Cara was using was staffed by high school kids from the Future Farmers of America. They still wore the same jackets they had when Amberley had been a member in high school. She'd also done 4-H. She bought a couple of caramel apples and met Cara's boyfriend, who was clearly smitten. They were cute. It seemed easy for them to be together.

Unlike Amberley, who always seemed to find the rockiest path to happiness with a man. Whatever that was about.

"See you on Monday, Cara," Amberley said leaving the booth and carrying her bag of goodies with her.

The pumpkin patch had an area at the front set up for pictures and she saw the kids lined up for photos. She walked past them, head down and focused on getting what she needed and getting home. She was going to give herself the rest of the day off. Maybe stop at the diner in town and grab some junk food and then go home, sit on the couch and binge-watch something on Netflix. Anything that would take her mind off the place where she kept going back to.

The missing family that she craved.

Will.

Screw Will.

He was clearly messed up from his wife's death. She got that. She could even understand what he must be going through. She was pretty damn sure he hadn't married a woman and had a kid with her if he didn't love her. That just didn't strike her as the kind of man he was. It was going to take him time to get over it. Obviously more than a year and she didn't begrudge him that.

She was angry at herself. She'd spent way too much time thinking about him. She should be thinking about one of the guys she'd met at the Wild Boar, or maybe one of the guys she'd met at the rodeo. Or no guy.

Maybe she'd just start collecting cats and build herself a nice life surrounded by animals and friends. Sure she'd miss having a man in her bed, but she could deal with that. Eventually.

She picked out five pumpkins to decorate her porch and two for the house—she had two windows that would look good with jack-o'-lanterns in them. And then she paid for a large bag of mini gourds and accepted the help of a pumpkin-patch employee to carry them all to her truck.

She carried the last pumpkin herself after three trips to the truck and was feeling much better about her day as she pulled into the diner. She'd phoned in her order so all she had to do was go in and grab it. She hopped out of her truck and walked straight to the counter to pick up her order when she heard someone call her name.

Will.

She turned to see him sitting at a corner table with Max St. Cloud. Though she'd only seen him in town, she knew Max on sight. And she tried to smile and wave, but she was just still so pissed.

She hadn't realized how much she'd been counting on him to be different from every other city guy she'd ever met. She settled for a little wave as the girl at the register called her name. She walked over and paid for her patty melt, fries and onion rings and then turned to walk out of the diner without looking over at Will.

One of them had to be smart and no matter how country she was, she knew it was up to her.

Five

"What was that about?" Max asked Will as they watched Amberley walk out of the diner.

"Nothing."

"Will, talk to me," Max said. "Did I make a mistake when I asked you to come to Royal?"

"No. It is not affecting my work. In fact, I think I am getting close to finding the hub that Maverick is using to run most of the cyberbullying he's doing. He uses a bunch of different accounts, but they are all fed from the same source...or at least that's what I'm starting to suspect."

Max sat back in the bench and nodded. "Good. But I wasn't referring to your work. You have been sending me reports at all hours of the day with updates."

"Then what are you asking?" Will was trying to focus on the conversation with his boss, but he couldn't keep his mind from wandering to Amberley.

"We're friends, right?" Max asked.

"Yeah. But unless you want to hear about what a sad mess I've become you should lay off this questioning right now," Will warned his friend. Max had known him before he'd married Lucy. He was one of the few people who really knew him well enough to understand what he'd gone through when he'd lost Lucy. How marriage had changed him and how her death had sent him to a darker place.

"What's up?"

"Nothing. Just the mix of pretty girl, messed-up guy and trying to do the right thing," Will said.

He took a sip of his coffee and leaned forward because he didn't need everyone in the diner to hear his business. "For the love of me, Max, every damn time I try to do what I know is right it backfires."

"Then stop trying," Max said.

"If it was that easy," Will said.

"It is. You said that you tried to do the right thing and it backfired. Maybe it was the wrong action," Max said. "All I know is that life isn't like a program. You fix the code and make it work, but there is always something unexpected. You know?"

Will leaned back. Like Lucy dying in the hospital after Faye's birth. "Yeah. I do know. Thanks, Max."

Max nodded. "People are getting more tense as this Maverick remains at large. I know you are doing all you can, but right now, because no one knows who Maverick is, everyone suspects each other. If you can get me something…well, the sooner the better."

"I will. Like I mentioned I think I have a lead on something that should lead to Maverick. I just needed to understand the server set up at the Texas Cattle-man's Club."

"I put you on the guest list so you can go check it out."

"Thanks. I want to add the access tracking to the main terminal and the server. I'm pretty sure it's got to be an inside job."

"I think there is a connection there, too," Max said. "So you don't want anyone to know why you are there."

"Yeah."

"A date would be good camouflage."

"Of course it would," Will said.

"Just trying to help a buddy out. You look like you need a nudge toward her."

"Thanks… Not a nudge. I need to get out of my own way. Every time I'm around her I forget things… Lucy. And then when I'm alone I'm not sure that's what I should have done."

"Only you can answer that for yourself, but you can't keep punishing yourself for living," Max said. "I'm going to ask Chelsea to make you a dinner res-ervation at the club for tonight. Get a date or not—it's up to you."

They discussed how Will would deploy the tracker physically on the server. They didn't want to do it re-motely, in case Maverick was able to see the code in the program. Max and he parted company and instead of heading back to the Flying E, Will went to one of the boutiques in town and bought a gauzy dress in a small flower print for Amberley. The dress had a skirt that he suspected would end just above her knee and a scooped neckline. He also purchased a pretty necklace that had a large amber gemstone pendant in the center that would rest nicely above the neckline of the dress.

He had it wrapped and then wrote a note of apology on the card and asked for it to be delivered to her.

He checked his watch and then went to the Fall Festival to meet Erin and Faye. Faye looked cute as could be in her denim overalls and brown undershirt. He held his daughter and knew that he'd be mad as hell if he'd been the one to die and Lucy was hesitating to get on with her life.

But it was harder on the heart than it was on the head. And as much as he knew what he needed to do, it was like Max had said—this wasn't code that he could correct with a few strokes of the keyboard. It was so much easier and conversely more complicated than that. He had no idea what he was really going to do about Amberley, but he'd made a move today. No more backing away.

If Amberley gave him this third chance, he wasn't going to waste it.

When he got back to the ranch, he dropped off Erin and Faye at the guest house since it was Faye's nap time and then he got in the golf cart and drove over to the stables to look for Amberley.

She was running the barrels when he got there and he watched her move with the horse and knew that she was worth the risk he was taking. He had spent a lot of time pretending that he could walk away from her, but the truth was he knew he couldn't.

He wanted her.

Not just physically, though that was a big part of

it. He also wanted that joie de vivre that she seemed
to bring to him when he was around her.

He liked the man he could be when he thought of
spending time with her.

She noticed him and drew her horse to a stop. She
dismounted and walked over to the fence around the
barrels, and he went to meet her.

"What's your deal?"

She hadn't meant to sound so confrontational.
She'd gone back to the ranch and intended to waste
away the rest of the day in front of the television. But
instead she'd felt trapped in her house. She'd felt restless and edgy and just as she was about to leave, that
package from Will had arrived.

With a handwritten apology note and a gorgeous
dress and necklace. Who did something like that?

It was safe to say that no man she'd dated before
had made such a gesture. But Will was different. And
they had never dated. What had possessed him to do
such a thing?

She was tired of playing games. It didn't suit her.

"My deal?"

"Yeah. We shared a great kiss and I started to think
I could really like this guy and then you just up and
disappear, not even a word about not showing up for
our scheduled ride. You must think all country girls
are just looking for a big-city man to marry them
and take them away from all this, but you're wrong.
I like this life. I like it just the way it is, and when
I kissed you it was because I thought we had a real
connection," she said, opening the gate and stepping
out of the ring. "And it's clear to me that we have

absolutely no connection at all by the way you keep backing out of stuff, but then you send me that dress and necklace and that apology. It sounds heartfelt, Will. And I'm tired of feeling stupid because I think one thing and your actions say something else. So what's your deal?"

He rocked back on his heels, as if he was trying to absorb the force of her aggression. She knew she was being hostile right now but she was tired of feeling the fool. The way he had treated her, the way she'd interpreted his actions…well, she wasn't having it anymore. She'd been nice and if he went to Clay and complained, she knew Clay well enough that she'd be honest with him and she was pretty sure he'd side with her.

"I am sorry. The note was meant to be heartfelt," he said, holding his hands up to his shoulders. "I like you, Amberley. When we are together I forget about the emptiness that I usually feel when I step away from my computer. But then I hold Faye and it comes back. I'm trying to get out of the swamp that I've been trapped in since Lucy died. And I can't figure it out. I'm not playing a game with you. I promise. I was going to invite you to dinner, but on second thought—"

"Do you really want to have dinner with me?" she asked, cutting him off. His explanation made her sad for him. She could feel his pain when he spoke. She, of all people, understood how hard it was to move on after a tragic loss. She could be his friend. Just his friend. That was something she could handle.

"Yes. I do."

"Okay, then let's have dinner. But as friends. We

can be friends, right?" she asked. "You can tell me about Lucy and maybe we can figure out a way to get you free of your swamp. It doesn't have to be anything more than that."

She could be his friend. Sure, she had wanted more, but the last few days had convinced her that wasn't wise. The anger and the despair from his rejection hadn't been what she'd expected. She had uncovered something buried deep inside her that she didn't like.

She wanted to celebrate being young and alive. Not feel old and bitter. She'd never been bitter about the hand that life had dealt her and she hated that this thing she felt for Will was eliciting that response in her.

"Friends?"

"Yes. Seems like a good place to start."

"Okay. Friends. Then I should tell you that I need a date for cover. I want to install a program on the server at the Texas Cattleman's Club, and in case it's an inside job, I don't really want anyone to know what I'm doing."

"So I'm your cover?"

"That's the plan, but I would also like it to be a date," he said. "I am tired of where I am and would like to get to a better place."

Sure, he would. As friends, she reminded herself. "I can do that. And I can provide some cover for you. What time is dinner?"

"Eight. That gives me time to spend with Faye before she goes to bed," he said.

"That works for me. How is she? I really enjoyed playing with her the other night."

"She's good. A little cranky earlier today, but that's just from teething. She's already got one tooth so this is another new one. She bit me last night when we were playing. She's been drooling a lot, so I was letting her chew on my finger and then *ouch*."

Amberley smiled at him like she would if he was a friend. She could do this. Keep her feelings on neutral terms. If only he wasn't so darn cute when he talked about his daughter.

He walked away and she turned her attention to her horse, brushing Montgomery and talking to the animal. He listened to her the way she suspected she'd listened to Faye. Montgomery lowered his head and butted her in the chest when she was done and she hugged him back, wishing she could understand men half as well as she understood horses.

Will took his time getting dressed for dinner after Erin and he had put Faye to bed. Erin was video chatting with her boyfriend back in Seattle, so he knew that she was set for the evening. He went into his office to check his computers again and took the small USB flash drive that he'd loaded his tracker program onto and put it in his pocket.

He was nervous.

He wasn't sure if that was a good thing or a bad thing. Faye always made him feel pretty okay…well, a little sad and bad that she didn't have her mom, but she had that sweet smile, which kind of helped to center him at times.

This was different. He went to the mirror in the guest bathroom and checked his tie again. He favored skinny ties no matter if they were in fashion or not.

He didn't think of himself as a slave to trends and preferred a look he thought worked for him. He'd spiked up his hair on the top and traded his Converse for some loafers his mom had sent him after her last trip to Italy.

He went in to check on Faye and kissed her on the top of her head before letting Erin know he was leaving for the evening.

He walked out of the house, took a deep breath of the fall evening air and realized how much he liked Texas. To be fair, October was a far cry from July, when he knew the temperature would be unbearable. But right now, this cool, dry night was exactly what he wanted.

He drove over to Amberley's house, having texted her earlier to tell her he'd pick her up. There was a bunch of pumpkins on her front step and a bale of hay with a scarecrow holding a sign that said Happy Fall, Y'all on it. He smiled as he saw it. He leaped up the stairs to her front porch and knocked on the door.

"It's open. Come in."

He did as she asked and stepped into the hallway of her place. The house smelled like apples and cinnamon, which reminded him of his parents' place. There was a thick carpeted runner in the foyer that led to the living room.

"I'll be right there. Sorry, I'm trying to curl my hair but it's being stubborn," she called out from the back of the house. "I am almost done."

"No problem," he said, following the sound of her voice. He found her standing in front of a mirror at the end of the hallway off the living room. He stopped when he saw her as his breath caught in his throat.

She was beautiful.

She'd looked pretty the other week after she'd been out, but this was different. Her hair had been pulled up into a chignon and that tendril she was messing with was curling against her cheek.

"Sorry. But in magazines this always looks so perfect and, of course, the reality is my stubborn hair won't curl the right way."

"I don't think it's a problem," he said.

She turned to face him and he had to swallow. The dress he'd picked out was fitted on the top and then flared out from her waist ending just above her knees. And she'd paired the dress with a pair of strappy sandals. The amber pendant fell on her chest, drawing his eyes to the V-neck of the dress.

"You are gorgeous," he said.

She blushed.

"Don't be embarrassed, it's just the truth," he said.

"Thanks for saying that. I don't get dressed up often, which is why I was trying this new updo. I figured I should at least make the effort. Plus, the folks of Royal aren't used to seeing me in anything but jeans and a straw cowboy hat. Do you think Maverick is working in the club or even a member…? Oh, that would really stink if he was a member, wouldn't it?"

"It would. I'm not a member, as you know, but I am aware of how close-knit the members are," Will said. "Are you ready to go?"

"Yes. Let me grab my purse and shawl. I figured that would be nicer than my jean jacket."

He smiled at the way she said it. She looked sophisticated and polished, almost out of his league, but she was still Amberley.

She disappeared into the doorway next to the hall mirror and reappeared a minute later. "Let's go."

He followed her through her home. It was small and neat, but very much Amberley. Not like the guest house, which was almost too perfectly decorated— this place had a more lived-in quality. It was her home. "How long have you lived here?"

"I got the job when I was nineteen…so that's five years."

"Wow, you were young. Were you worried about moving away from home?" he asked.

"Not really. Dad and Clay have known each other for a while. And it's not like it's that far if I want to go home for a visit," she said. "Plus Clay has an ex- cellent stable and he lets me have time off to rodeo when I want to—it's the best place for me."

She was animated when she spoke of her father and her job and her life, and he realized he wanted to see her like this always.

She'd suggested they be friends and he knew now that was the only route for the two of them. Because he wanted her to stay the way she was just now. With her skin glowing, her eyes animated as she talked about the things in her life she loved. Getting in- volved with him could only bring her down. And even though he knew he felt like he was missing out on something special, her smile and her happiness was worth it.

Six

The Texas Cattleman's Club dining room was busy when they arrived. Since Maverick had started his assault on members of the club, and on Royal, some of the friendliness that Amberley had always associated with the town was gone. Everyone was a little bit on edge. She wasn't going to pretend she understood what Will was doing with the computer, but she'd Googled him and read up on him.

They were dining as guests of Chelsea Hunt and she'd met them early at the bar.

If anyone could unearth Maverick it was Will Brady. He was a whiz at tracking down cyber criminals and had made millions selling the code he had designed to the US government. He was gaining a reputation for keeping secrets safe as well, having successfully blocked an all-out assault on one government database by a foreign entity intent on doing harm to the US. Obviously, Will was a well-respected expert in his field.

One of the articles had been accompanied by a picture of him and his late wife dressed up to go to the White House, where Will had been given a commendation.

Seeing that picture of Will's late wife had made the woman very real to Amberley. And she was even more glad she'd decided just to be friends with Will. She liked him. She wasn't going to pretend otherwise. As she went to the bar while he excused himself to go do whatever he had to do in the computer room, she thought more about all Will had lost.

She wanted to be a good friend to Will. He needed a friend.

She remembered how he'd made up a story for her while they'd sat under the stars. No one had done that for her since she was a girl. The men she had dated…they saw the tough cowgirl and they didn't always realize she was vulnerable. But Will treated her differently.

"What'll it be?" the bartender asked her.

"Strawberry margarita, frozen, please," she said.

"Should I open a tab?" the bartender asked.

"No. I'll pay for this. I'm having dinner with someone," she said.

She settled up with the bartender, took her drink to one of the high tables and sat down to wait. She saw a few people she knew from town, but they glanced over her as if they didn't recognize her and she shook her head. She didn't think she looked so different with her hair up.

Finally, one of the parents of her horse-riding students recognized her and came over to chat with her for a few moments. It was nice to have someone to talk to while she was waiting for Will. She felt a little bit out of place here at the club. She didn't come from money. Her father made a good living and the ranch was worth a fair amount, but they weren't wealthy. They were ranchers.

Will walked in a few minutes later and scanned the room before spotting her. He smiled, buttoning his coat as he strode over to her. He looked good in his thin tie and his slim-fitting suit. His hair was slicked back, making him look like he'd just stepped out of one those television shows she loved to binge-watch.

She sighed.

Friends, she reminded herself.

"I didn't order you a drink," she said, wishing now she had.

"That's okay. I'll get one and join you," he said.

He was back in a moment, sitting across from her with a whiskey in one hand. "Sorry to keep you waiting."

"I don't mind. Did you get everything straightened out?"

"I did," he said. "How has it been for you?"

"Funny," she said. "I've seen a few people from town but most didn't recognize me."

"Really?"

"Yup. I'm a woman of mystery," she said. "I like it."

"Me, too. It's nice to be anonymous," he said.

"Are you usually recognized?" she asked. "I read a few articles about you online."

"Did you?" he asked. "That's interesting. But to answer your question, I'm only recognized at home. Mainly it's because I don't live that far from where I grew up. One subdivision over, actually, so I just know everyone when I go to the gym or the grocery store. And most people know about Lucy so it makes things awkward…"

She put her hand over his.

"Do you want to talk about her?" Amberley asked. "When my mom died everyone stopped mentioning her name. It was like she'd never existed and I wanted to talk about her. Finally, one night I lit into my daddy about it. And he said he missed her so much just hearing her name hurt and I told him for me, too, but ignoring her was making her disappear," Amberley said, feeling the sting of tears as she remembered her mom. She'd been gone for years now, but there were times like this when she still missed her and it felt fresh.

"I…I'm a little bit of both. I don't know if I want to talk about her," Will admitted. He took his hand from under hers and swallowed his drink in one long gulp.

"If you want to, I'm here for you," she said.

He nodded. "I'm going to go and check on our table."

She watched him walk away and she wondered if she'd said too much. But she knew that she couldn't have kept silent. He had admitted to her that he was stuck in a swamp and there was no clear path out of it. She suspected it was because he didn't know how to move on and still hold on to the past. And while Amberley knew she was no expert, she'd done her best to keep her mom alive while accepting the woman her dad had started dating when she'd turned eighteen.

So maybe she'd be able to help him.

Dinner started out a little stiff but soon they relaxed into a good conversation, mostly centering on music and books. They differed in that everything he owned was digital—both books and music—while Amberley had inherited her mother's record collection when she'd moved out and had a turntable in her house, where she listened to old country and rock from the '80s.

"What about scratches?"

"Well, that does make for some awkward moments when I'm singing along to a song that I've learned with all the skips in it. Records do that," she said with a wink. "And then I realize there's an entire phrase I've missed."

"You know I could show you how to download all the albums you already own on your phone so you could listen to them when you are riding," he said.

"I know how to do that, Will," she said. "I just prefer to listen to the albums at home. It reminds me of when I was growing up. Like Mom loved Michael Bolton and when I listen to his album I can remember Dad coming and the two of them dancing around. And I have a lot of CDs, too. Between the two of them I think they owned every album they loved on cassette, CD and vinyl. It's crazy," she said. "Dad stopped listening to it all after Mom died, but I wanted my brothers and sisters to have those memories, so Randy and I would put the albums on when Dad was out of the house."

"How many siblings do you have?"

"Four. Two brothers and two sisters. Randy is three years younger than me, then Janie, Michael and Tawny."

"Sounds like a houseful," he said. He'd always sort of wished for a bigger family but he'd been the only child and had gotten used to it.

"What about you?" she asked.

"Only child."

"Spoiled," she said, winking at him.

"Probably," he admitted. "Lucy and I had planned to have at least two kids. She said we should have an even number—she had two sisters and said one of them was always left out."

"It was that way at home a bit when Mom was still alive, but once she died and I became the boss when Dad wasn't home the dynamic changed."

"How old were you?" he asked.

"Thirteen," she said. "You know you could always have more kids if you remarry."

"Uh, I'm barely able to think about going on a date, I'm not sure more kids are in the cards for me," he said. "What about you? Do you hate the idea of being a mom since you kind of had to be one to your siblings?"

She sat back in her chair and tucked that tendril she'd spent so much time trying to curl behind her ear. She shook her head. "No. I sort of always wanted to have a family of my own."

There was something in the way she was talking that made him think she thought she wouldn't have a family of her own. "You're young. You can have a family someday."

She chewed her lower lip for a minute and then shook her head. "I can't. I physically can't have kids."

He was surprised and wanted to ask her more about it, but it seemed obvious to him that she didn't want to discuss it further. She started eating her dinner again and this time didn't look up.

He reached over and put his hand on top of hers, stopping her from taking another bite, and she looked up. There was pain in her eyes and it echoed the loss he felt in his soul when he thought about Lucy being gone.

"I'm sorry."

She nodded. "Thanks. Wow, I bet you're glad this isn't a real date."

"It is a real date," he said. Because he knew now that there was no way he could walk away from her. Yes, he had been hesitating, but when he'd bought the dress for her things had changed and he wasn't going to let it go back to where he'd been when he'd first come to Texas.

"No, we said friends."

"Friends can go on dates. How else do you think friends become lovers?"

She flushed. He loved her creamy complexion and the fact that her face easily broadcast her emotions. He guessed it went hand-in-hand with her bluntness. Amberley didn't hide any part of who she was.

"I can't deal if you are going to blow hot and cold again," she said. "I wasn't kidding around this afternoon. I mean, I understand where you are coming from—"

"Amberley? I told Chris that was you," Macy Richardson said, coming over to her. Macy's family had been members of the Texas Cattleman's Club forever. Chris had grown up here in Royal on the wrong sides of the tracks. But he'd gone away and made his fortune, only to come back to claim Macy and a membership at the club. Their daughter took riding lessons from Amberley.

"It is me," she said. "Probably didn't recognize me without my cowboy hat on. Macy and Chris, this is Will Brady. He's a guest of Chelsea Hunt's."

Will stood up and shook Macy's and Chris's hands. "I hear you're in town to help catch Maverick."

"I am," Will said.

"Good. I'm sure you're going to get the job done. Chelsea has a lot of good things to say about you," Macy said. "We will leave you to your dinner."

A few other members stopped by to chat with them, including Clay and Sophia, who seemed to be enjoying their night out.

When the interruptions were over, Will picked up the thread of their conversation. Amberley's accusations about his behavior were fair, and he owed her a response.

"You're right. I'm not going to do that to you again. I said friends to lovers. We can take this slow," he said.

But a part of him knew that slow was going to be hard with her. It almost felt like if it happened in a rush it would be easier for him to move past the memory of Lucy, but as he watched Amberley he knew that he was always moving forward. He was excited about the prospect of something fresh and new with her. He wasn't about to give up now that he had her. He could do slow, but he wouldn't do never.

"So books… Do you have a bunch of dog-eared paperbacks instead of ebooks?" he asked, changing the subject and trying to pretend like everything was normal.

"Dog-eared? I love my books—I don't treat them poorly. In fact, sometimes I buy the paperback and then read it on my tablet because I want to keep it in good shape," she admitted.

He had to laugh at the way she said it and then he noticed how she smiled when he laughed. Something shifted and settled inside of him and he realized that he wasn't going to let her ride out of his life until he knew her much better.

Will drove her home at the end of the night, playing a new track he'd downloaded of Childish Gambino. It had a funky sound that reminded her of some of the jazzy music her dad liked from the '80s.

"This is really interesting. I love it," she said.

"I thought you might like it," he said.

"Why?"

"Because I do and we seem to have similar taste in music," he said.

"You think so?"

He nodded. "Tonight I have learned we are more alike than either of us would have guessed."

She swallowed hard—he meant the loss. It was funny that grief should unite them, but then her grandmother always said her mom was up there watching out for her, so maybe that was the reason behind this.

"Were you surprised?" she asked.

"Yes, and shame on me for that. Because from

the moment you showed up on my front porch with Cara, I knew you weren't like any other woman I'd met before. A part of me put it down to you being a Texan, but I knew there was something about you that was just different from every other woman," he said.

"Well, not everyone can be born in the great state of Texas," she said with a wink. "You can't really hold that against other women."

He laughed, as she hoped he would. She noticed that he got her sometimes odd sense of humor and it made her feel good. As much as she'd sort of always crushed out city guys that she'd met, he was different. Maybe that was why she kept giving him a second chance.

"I wouldn't," he said solemnly.

"So do you have any country music on your device?"

"Big and Rich," he said.

"They're okay but I think you need to listen to some old-school country. I'll give you some of Dad's old cassettes," she said, again teasing him because she knew he would just download the songs. And he was right that some songs sounded better digitally remastered, but for the sake of not agreeing with him she was going to stick by her guns.

He groaned. "Just give me a list. Actually, give me a name and I'll put it on right now."

"How?"

"Verbal commands," he said.

"Does that work for you?" she asked.

"All the time. Why?"

"Well, Siri hates me. Whatever I say she changes

it to something crazy. I mean, it's not like I'm not speaking English," she said.

"Siri can't hate you, she's a computer program," Will said.

"Well, she does. One time I texted my cousin Eve and told her where to meet me and do you know what that phone sent her?"

"What?" he asked.

"'Meet me where we once flew the summer wind,'" Amberley said.

He burst out laughing. "You do have a bit of an accent."

"No crap," she said. "But that is crazy."

"When we get to your place I'll fix it so your phone can understand you," he said.

"You can do that?"

"Hell, yes," he said. "I might not be any good with people but I'm excellent with tech."

She looked over at him, his features illuminated whenever they passed under a streetlamp as they drove through Royal. "You're good with people."

"Some of them. I tend to lose my patience. But with tech I'm always good."

She hadn't seen that impatient side of him. She wondered if that was because he was only letting her see what he wanted. Maybe the grieving widower was all he wanted her to know about him. But then why would he be talking to her now? She was making herself a little crazy.

They had both been beat up by life and were doing their best to survive. And she didn't doubt that he liked her. She'd seen the way he watched her and she knew when a man wanted her.

The truth was she didn't want to be hurt again and her mind might have been saying that friends was enough for her, but she knew in her heart that she'd already started liking him.

She liked that he cared about Royal even though it wasn't his town. She liked the way he was with his daughter, even though raising her without his mother was obviously hurting him. She just plain liked him and that wasn't how she wanted to be feeling about him.

Friends.

That was easy. She was supposed to be keeping things friendly. Instead she was falling for him.

It would have been easier if she knew that he would stay, but he was a flight risk. She knew he was just tiptoeing through an emotional minefield, trying to figure out how to move on. And of course once Maverick was found there was no reason for Will to stay in Texas. And then she shifted things in her mind. What if he was a mustang stallion that just took a little longer to gentle to the saddle? What if she just approached him with stealth, could she win him that way?

And was she really going to try to win him over?

She twisted her head and looked out at the dark landscape as they left Royal and headed toward the Flying E. She saw the moon up there following her and then she spotted Venus and thought of her own special angel, and not for the first time in her adult life, she wished her mom was here to talk to. She needed some advice on what to do next. She wasn't someone to hedge her bets and she wanted to be all in with Will. But a part of her was afraid that it was just wishful thinking on her part.

He turned onto the Flying E property and slowed the car, as they were on the dirt road and not paved highway. When he stopped in front of her house she turned to face him.

He shut off the car and sat there for a long moment and she felt a tingle go through her entire body that wasn't unlike what she felt when she was sitting on the back of Montgomery waiting for a barrel run to start.

"So, you want to come in?"

Seven

The dinner hadn't gone as Will had expected and this end to the evening was no different. He'd told himself he wouldn't kiss her good-night. They'd said they'd go slow. Maybe if he repeated it enough times it would stick and he'd get the taste of her off his tongue.

Unfortunately, he was never going to get the vision of her wearing the gauzy, long-sleeved dress he'd bought for her out of his mind. And it didn't help matters that the hem of her dress had ridden up her legs. In the light of the moon and the illumination of the dashboard lights he could see the tops of her thighs.

He clenched his hands around the steering wheel to keep from reaching over and touching her. Lust was strong and sharp and it was burning out all the cells in his brain, making it impossible for him to think. He wanted to be suave and smooth, all the things he liked to think he usually was around a woman, but tonight he wasn't.

He'd told her things he'd never said to anyone else. Like making up stories under the stars and just talking about stuff. Not business or his baby, but stuff that he'd locked away when Lucy died. And all the sophistication he'd thought he'd cultivated over the years was gone. He wanted her and really there wasn't room for anything else. Maybe it was the way she'd watched him as he'd driven back to the ranch.

Hell, he didn't know.

Frankly, he didn't care.

"You really want me to come in?" he asked, his voice sounding rough. He cleared it but he knew short of burying himself hilt-deep between her legs there was nothing he could do about it.

"Do you want to come in?" she asked.

"Hell."

She turned in her seat and the fabric of the dress was pulled taut against the curves of her breasts and he could only stare at her body as she leaned in close. A wave of her perfume surrounded him and now he knew he wasn't leaving.

He reached across the gearbox in the middle of the two bucket seats and wrapped his hand around the back of her head. He slid his fingers along the back of her neck, and his hand brushed against the part where she'd twisted up her hair—he wanted it free and flowing around her shoulders but right now he wanted her mouth more.

He needed to feel her lips under his. To prove to himself that lust had addled his thinking. That there was no way she tasted as good as he remembered. She couldn't.

No woman could taste like sin and heaven at the same time.

He tried to justify this kiss just to prove to himself that it had been the absence of kissing in the past year that had made hers unforgettable.

But as he leaned in closer, watching as her lips parted and her tongue darted out to wet her lips, he knew that was a lie. There was a jolt of pure sexual need that went through him and his erection stirred, pressing tight against his pants. He wanted to shift to relieve some of the pressure but he needed the pain to keep him grounded. To remind himself this wasn't a fantasy but something that was truly happening.

Now.

He brushed his lips over hers and her hand came up to rest against his chest. Her fingers moved under his tie to the buttons of his shirt and slipped through. She brushed the tip of one finger over his skin just as he thrust his tongue deep into her mouth. She moaned, shifting on the seat to scoot closer to him. He felt her arms wrap around his neck and shoulders as she drew herself closer to him. He grabbed her waist, squeezing her as he caressed his way around to her back. She felt like a ball of fire in his arms. Like a mustang that was wild and would take him on the ride of his life if he could hold on long enough.

He had a feeling deep in his soul that he could never tame her.

Amberley was going to be the ride of his life, he knew that. And for a second the grief he'd shoved into a box before he'd gone out with her tonight tried to rear its ugly head, and in response he lifted his head and looked down into her face.

Her hair was starting to come loose from the chignon, thanks to his hands in her hair, and there was a flush on her face, her lips were parted. And her pretty brown eyes were watching him. A little bit with patience and a lot with need.

She needed this as much as he did.

Tonight had shown him that they were both broken in ways that the world would never see. He felt honored that she'd let him see the truth that was the real Amberley.

He put his forehead against hers, their breathing comingled as he wrapped both arms around her and lifted her from the seat. It took a little maneuvering and it wasn't comfortable at all, but he managed to move into the passenger seat and get her settled on his lap.

"That was…I didn't realize you were so strong," she said, softly.

"I'm not."

"You are. I'm not a lightweight," she said.

"Yes, you are. You are perfect," he said.

She put her fingers over his mouth. "Don't. I'm not perfect and you really don't think I am. No lies. This is…what we've both wanted since that moment in the field when you got off your horse. And I don't want to ruin it, but honesty…that has to be where this comes from."

He wanted that, too. Wanted this sweet Southern girl who was blunt and real and made him want things he wasn't sure he was ready for. But walking away wasn't going to happen.

He needed her.

But he didn't want to talk and if he was being honest with himself he didn't want to think at all.

Instead, he reached for the seat release and pushed it all the way back. She shifted around until she straddled him. He reached up and pulled the pins from her hair, then gently brought it forward until it hung in thick waves around her shoulders.

Carefully, slowly, he drew the fabric of the skirt part of her dress up to her waist until he could touch her thighs. They were smooth and soft but there was the underlying muscled hardness of her legs. She shifted against him, her hands framing his jaw as she tilted her head to the left. Her hair brushed against his neck as she lowered her mouth and sucked on his lower lip. She thrust her tongue deep into his mouth as she lowered her body against him.

And his pants were too tight. He reached between their bodies, his knuckles brushing against the crotch of her panties, and he felt the warmth of her there. But he focused on undoing his pants and sighed when he was free of the restriction of cloth.

He took her thigh in one hand and then squeezed, sliding his hand under the fabric of her panties and taking her butt in his hand. He drew her forward until she was rubbing over him.

He groaned and tore his mouth from hers.

He wanted to feel her naked against him.

"Shift up," he said.

"What?"

"I want to take your panties off."

She nodded, bracing herself on the seat behind him. She moved until he was able to draw her underwear down her legs and off. He tossed it on the driver's seat and then turned his attention to her breasts, which were in his face. He buried his head in her cleavage, turning his head to the left and dropping sweet kisses against her exposed flesh. She shivered and shifted her shoulders as she settled back on his lap, moving over him, and suddenly he didn't know how long he could last with her on top of him.

She was hot and wet and wanted him.

He found the zipper at the back of her dress and drew it down, and the bodice gaped enough for him to nudge the fabric aside until her breast was visible. She wore a demi bra that bared part of the full globe of her breast. He reached up and pulled the lacy fabric down until her nipple was visible and then leaned forward to suck it into his mouth. With his other hand, he caressed her back, drew his nail down the line of her spine to the small of her back, then cupped her butt and drew her forward again.

He encouraged her to move against him. She started to rock, rubbing her center over his shaft, and he felt a jolt at the base of his spine as his erection grew again.

He suckled harder on her nipple and she put her hands on his shoulders, rubbing against him with more urgency. He reached between their bodies, parting her until he could rub her clit with his finger. She groaned his name and put her hands in his hair, forcing his head back until her mouth fell on his. She thrust her tongue deep into his mouth, her tongue mimicking the movements of her hips.

He felt like he was about to explode and started dropping little nips all over the curves of both of her breasts and her neck. He tangled one hand in her hair as he traced the opening of her body, then pushed his finger slowly up into her.

She made a wild sound that just drove him higher and he thrust his finger up inside her, feeling her body tighten around it. Then he added a second finger and she shifted, until she had her hands braced on his shoulders. She rode him as fiercely as she'd ridden her horse as she chased the barrels in the ring.

He rubbed her with his thumb while continuing to thrust his fingers inside her and then she threw her head back and called his name in a loud voice as she shuddered in his arms before collapsing against him.

He kept his fingers in her body and wrapped his arm around her back, holding her to him. He was on the edge and wanted to come but a part of him wouldn't allow it. Giving her pleasure was one thing but taking it for himself was something he wasn't ready to do.

She shifted and he moved his fingers from her body. He was tempted to bring them to his mouth and lick them clean. Taste her in that intimate way. But he didn't. He felt her shift her hips and the tip of him was right there, poised at the entrance of her body.

He tightened his buttocks and shifted his hips without thinking, entering her without meaning to.

She felt so damn good. Her body wrapped tightly around his length. It was almost as if she was made for him.

She was tight and it was only as she shifted and he felt himself moving deeper into her that he realized what he was doing. He was in the front seat of his car, hooking up with Amberley.

Amberley.

He'd promised himself that he wasn't going to hurt her and he knew if he let this go any further...

He couldn't do it. He couldn't have sex with her and then lie in bed with her. He couldn't just take her on the front seat of his car. Their first time should be special.

He wanted to be better than he knew he was.

She tightened her inner muscles around him and he knew he was going to lose it right then. So he lifted her up and off him. Turned her on his lap so that she was seated facing to the side. Gingerly he reached for his underwear and tucked himself back into it. He was so on edge it would only take one or two strokes for him to come, but he wasn't going to do that.

Not now.

She deserved better than this. Bold and brash Amberley, who had always given him a kind of honesty that made him want to meet her more than halfway.

Now that his mind was back in the game and he wasn't being ruled by his hormones he realized that a part of him had chosen the front of the car because it wasn't the bedroom.

Like the bedroom was only for...

Lucy.

"Uh, what's going on here?" Amberley asked.

He couldn't talk right now. The only thing he was capable of saying would be a long string of her curse words. And she certainly didn't need to hear that.

"Will? It's okay. Whatever it is you're thinking, it's okay."

"It's not okay," he said.

She put her hands on his face and forced him to

look up at her. She leaned down and kissed him so softly and gently that he knew he didn't deserve to have her in his life.

"Yes, it is. Am I the first...since Lucy?"

He nodded. "It's not that I don't—"

"You don't have to explain," she said. "I am going to go into my house now."

He couldn't stop her even though a part of him wanted to. He wasn't ready to make love to a woman who wasn't his wife. It didn't matter that he knew Lucy was gone and that Amberley was sitting here looking more tempting that a woman had a right to.

He wasn't ready.

Damn.

He had a half-naked woman in his lap and he was about to let her walk away.

"I'm sorry," he said abruptly. There had been a lot of firsts since Lucy had died and he'd never thought about this situation. It had felt natural and right... and then it hadn't.

"Don't be. We're friends."

"Friends don't do what we just did," he said.

"Some of them do," she returned. "'Night, Will."

She opened the door and got out of the car, straightening the top of her dress. He reached out and caught her hand. Brought it to his lips and kissed the back of it. He wished he had words to tell her what this night meant to him. How she was changing him and the way he looked at life and himself, but he could only gaze up at her. She tugged her hand free and touched his lips before turning and walking away.

He watched her leave, knowing he should go after her. But he didn't. He just sat there for a few more minutes until he saw her door close and then he got out and walked around to the driver's side of the car and got in. He was breathing like he'd run a fifty-yard dash, then he put his head on the steering wheel, unable to move.

He was torn. His conscience said to go back home and sleep in his empty bed. Let the frustration he felt make sleep impossible because he deserved to suffer.

He was moving on when Lucy couldn't. But he knew that was survivor's guilt talking. He took a deep breath. But all he could smell was sex and Amberley, and he wanted her again. His mind might be preaching patience but his groin was saying to hell with that and to take what he needed. But he couldn't.

It wouldn't be right for Amberley.

He knew this was a first.

The therapist he'd seen after Lucy's death said each first was going to be like a milestone and everything would continue to get easier. Hell, it couldn't get any harder than this. But damn, when was that going to happen? He felt like Don Quixote tilting at windmills and not getting anywhere. He was chasing something that was always just out of reach. But for tonight— tonight he'd almost touched it.

He'd almost given himself permission to move on. But he wasn't ready. What if he never was? What if by the time he was, Amberley had given up on him? Was she the one?

She'd certainly felt like someone important as he'd held her in his arms. He wanted more from her. Wanted more for himself than he'd taken tonight. He just wasn't sure what kind of sign he was waiting for.

It wasn't like Lucy was going to tell him it was

okay to move on. She couldn't. He knew he was the only one who could decide when it was time.

Was it time?

Maybe it wasn't time that was the important thing, it was the person. And it had felt very right with Amberley.

He finally felt like he'd settled down enough to drive back to the guest house he was staying in. As he got out of the car, he fastened his pants and then looked down and saw her panties on his seat.

He lifted them up, tucked them into his pocket and walked into the house feeling like a man torn in two. A man with both the past and the future pulling at him.

He didn't know what he was going to have with Amberley, but as he walked into the house and locked up behind him, he realized that Erin had left a light on for him and he went down the hall to Faye's bedroom.

He looked down on his sleeping little girl and felt that punch in the heart, as he knew he had to make sure that she didn't lose both her mom and her dad that day that Lucy had died. He knew that she deserved to have a father who was participating in life, not one who was locked away in his office and spending his days and nights in the cyberworld because he was afraid to live in the real one.

He leaned over the side of the crib and kissed her forehead.

And he could only hope that Amberley had meant it when she said she forgave him for tonight because he wasn't done with that cowgirl yet.

Eight

Amberley didn't sleep well that night. She wasn't a heartless monster—she understood where Will was coming from. And when they were at dinner at the club she'd realized that he was going to take some extra time if they were going to be more than friends. And being friends…well, how could she not be his friend.

She was hurt. She didn't hook up and sleep around, not anymore. She had found a place for herself where she'd started to adjust to her life. She'd begun to feel like she'd found a peace that had always been just out of reach. Then Will Brady showed up, arousing feelings from her past and reawakening the passion she'd thought she'd buried a long time ago.

But as she stared down at her breakfast cereal she knew she had wanted some kind of romantic fantasy.

That was the problem with watching as much television as she did and reading as many books. There
were times when she just wanted her life to have a
little more romance than it did.

Last night in his car, Will had made her feel things
that she hadn't ever felt before. It had been more intense than the other times she'd had sex.

She wasn't really eating her cereal so she carried
the bowl to the sink, and even though she knew she
should clean it out right now, she just dumped the
bowl in the sink, rinsed the cereal down the drain
and then left it.

She had told Clay that she'd break in one of the
newer horses and she intended to use Sunday morning
to do it. She had a lesson this afternoon and then she
needed to keep practicing her barrel riding, as she was
signed up for a rodeo at the beginning of November.

But this morning all she had to do was get Squire
ready for riding and lessons. The hands mostly had
their own horses or used some of the saddle horses
that Clay kept on the ranch. And Amberley's job was
to make sure they were all in good shape and exer-
cised if they weren't being used.

She heard some sounds coming from the stall set
away from the other animals at the end of the stables
and turned in that direction. She saw Sophie, Clay's
pregnant wife, standing outside the stall talking to
the bull inside of it.

"Sophie? Everything okay?" Amberley asked as
she walked down toward her.

The stall held Iron Heart…the very same bull that
had ended Clay's bull-riding career. Clay had saved

the animal from being euthanized and brought him to the Flying E ranch.

"Yeah, just talking about stubbornness with someone who understands it."

Amberley had to laugh. "Clay."

Sophie nodded. "You'd think I was the first woman to ever be pregnant."

Babies again. It seemed that no matter how hard she tried she couldn't get away from pregnancy or babies. "I think it's sweet how protective he is."

"Well, that's probably because you're not the one being smothered," Sophie said with a small smile.

"I was once the one being ignored and told not to have a baby," Amberley said. She hadn't meant to. She was pretty sure that no one here knew about her past except her doctor in town.

"Oh, Amberley, I'm so sorry. Did you—"

"No. I had a miscarriage," Amberley said. "Gosh, I don't know why I'm telling you all this. I guess just to say that having Clay dote on you is a very good thing."

"I agree. Just wish he wasn't so stubborn all the time."

Amberley knew exactly how Sophie felt. "Aren't all men?"

"They are," Sophie said and then waved goodbye as she left the barn.

Amberley went back to Squire's stall, brushed and saddled the horse and then took him out for a ride. But she wasn't alone. Not in her mind. She remembered the way that Will had ridden when she'd taken him out here. She remembered how he'd looked when he'd gotten off his horse and looked up at her. Asked her for something she hadn't wanted to give him at the time.

Now she was wondering if that had been a mistake.

She was trying not to feel cheap and used. She'd meant it last night when she'd said she understood him calling things off. She had. She couldn't imagine the emotions he was going through as he tried to process his grief and move on from losing his wife. She only could funnel it through her experiences of losing her mom and of losing…

She shook her head to shove that thought away and focused on the ride. Squire wasn't really in the mood to run and when Amberley tried to force the issue he bucked and she hung on the first time, but when he did it again, she was knocked off and fell to the ground, landing hard on her shoulder.

Angry at herself for being distracted, she got up and took Squire's reins and started walking back to the stables. But the horse nudged her shoulder and she looked into those eyes and decided he was ready for another chance. She got back in the saddle and they took a leisurely gallop across the field, and she suddenly stopped thinking as she leaned low over Squire and whispered to him. Told him how he was born to run and that she was only here to guide him.

She had one of those moments where everything shifted inside her. Maybe it had been being bucked off the back of the horse that had shaken her and made her see things differently.

But she knew she couldn't keep doing everything in the exact same way. Squire liked being talked to. It had been a long time since she'd had a horse that needed to hear her voice. Mostly she communicated with clicks of her tongue and the movement of her thighs.

She realized that Will was like Squire and last night…well, last night he'd bucked her off, but if she was careful she could find a way to get him back into the stable. She shook her head.

Did she want to work that hard for a man whose life was somewhere else?

She drew in a sharp breath and realized that it didn't matter where his life was, he was going to be one big ol' regret if she didn't do everything she could to claim him. That she wasn't going to be able to just walk away. But she'd known that.

That was the reason why she'd said just to be friends even knowing there was no way she'd ever be satisfied with less than everything he had to give.

Last night he'd taken the first step in moving out of the past. She was willing to give him a little breathing room, but she wasn't going to let him retreat again.

She got back to the barn and stabled Squire and then went to her place to shower and change. She found that there was a note taped to her front door. She opened it.

Amberley,
    Thank you for an incredible evening. I'd like to take you out to dinner tonight. Please be ready at seven. Wear something glamorous.
Will

This was the romance she'd been wishing for. And as she opened her front door and went to her bedroom to try to find the right dress, she knew that he wasn't running this time. And her heart did that little fluttery thing when she thought about him.

Will had taken care of everything for his date with Amberley. In the meantime, he was busy at his computer. The program he'd loaded onto the server at the Texas Cattleman's Club was spitting out all kinds of data and Will focused on analyzing it.

Erin had gone to town to run an errand and Faye was sitting on his lap chewing on one of her teething toys and babbling to herself as she liked to do while he worked. He squeezed his little girl closer to him as he continued working. A few articles popped up that he hadn't read before.

One was about a recluse who seemed to have a beef with just about everyone in Royal. Adam Haskell.

The reason his name had come up in the database was that he had written several strongly worded letters to the members of the town commission as well as local business owners. He might not leave his house very often, but he was very active online using Yelp and other local forums to criticize most of Royal. Will used his smartpen to send the articles and the name to Max to get his feedback. Perhaps his friend would have more intel on Haskell.

Faye shifted around on his lap and he turned to set her on the floor. She crawled toward the big plastic keyboard he'd picked up for her in town recently and then shifted to her feet and took two wobbling steps.

She walked.

His baby girl…

She dropped back down and started crawling

again. Will forgot the computers and got down on the floor.

"Faye, come to Daddy," he said.

She looked at him and gave him that drooly grin of hers and then turned and crawled to him.

The doorbell rang and he scooped Faye into his arms and carried her with him as he went to answer it.

Amberley.

"Hi," she said. "I wasn't sure how I was supposed to let you know I was available for our date tonight."

"I thought you'd text."

"Oh, sorry," she said. "I was here so I thought I'd just stop by."

"It's okay. Want to come in?" he asked, stepping back so she could enter. Faye was already smiling and babbling at Amberley.

"If you're not busy," Amberley said.

"I'm not busy. But this one just took two wobbling steps. Want to see if you can help me get her to walk?" he asked.

"Did she?" Amberley asked. "I'd love to help."

He carried Faye into the living room and then he was kind of at a loss. He placed her on the ground and she crawled around and then sat up and looked at him.

"Let me help. You sit over there," Amberley said, scooping Faye up and moving a few feet from him. Then she set Faye down on her feet and held Faye's hands in each of hers.

Faye wobbled a bit and Will realized he wanted to get this on camera.

"Wait. Let me set up my camera. I don't want to miss this," he said.

"Go ahead. We are going to practice, aren't we?"

Amberley asked, squatting down next to Faye and talking to her.

She smiled at Faye and Will watched the two of them together. They were cute, his girls, but he didn't let himself dwell too much on that. Instead he got his camera set up so that he would be able to capture the entire walk from one side of the room to the other. Then he went back to sit down so his baby could walk to him.

"Okay, I'm ready," Will said.

"Are *you* ready?" Amberley asked Faye.

She wobbled and Amberley let Faye hold on to her fingers and she started moving slowly, taking one step and then another. Will hit the remote so that the camera would start recording. Amberley let go of one of Faye's hands, and then the other, and his daughter smiled at him as she started walking toward him.

He clapped his hands and called her and she came right to him. He felt tears stinging his eyes as he lifted her into his arms, hugging her and praising her for doing a good job.

"She's such a rock star," Amberley said.

"Sit down," Will said. "Let's see if she will walk back to you."

Amberley did. "Faye, come to me."

Will set her on her feet and steadied her, then she took off again in that unsteady gait, walking to Amberley, who kept talking to her the entire time.

She scooped Faye up when she got to her and kissed the top of her head and Will realized that he'd found someone special in Amberley. She had a big heart and she deserved a man who would cherish that heart and give her the family she'd always craved. He wanted to believe he could be that man but he still had his doubts.

They spent another half hour letting Faye walk back and forth between them until Erin got back home.

"Look what Faye has mastered," Will said. "Amberley, go over there."

She did and they got Faye set up to walk over to her and Will noticed a look on Erin's face that he'd never seen before. It was almost as if she was disappointed that she hadn't been here for Faye's first steps. And suddenly he realized this was the first milestone in Faye's life that he hadn't shared with Erin.

"Sorry you missed her first steps," Will said. "I recorded it, though. She's so eager to go."

"She is. She's growing up so fast," Erin said.

"Yes, she is," Will agreed.

"Well, I'll leave you two alone," Erin said. "Are you still going out tonight?"

"Yes, I'm going out with Amberley."

"Oh, that's nice," Erin said.

Amberley left a few minutes later because she still had a lot to do, but Will felt deep inside that something had changed between them and he couldn't help getting his hopes up.

Amberley wasn't sure what she'd expected but the limousine Will pulled up in wasn't it. Will wore a dinner jacket and formal shirt and bow tie. He had his hair spiked and there was excitement and anticipation in those forest green eyes of his. She'd twisted her hair up and tonight the style and her hair seemed to be on the same page.

The dress she'd picked was a fitted dress in a deep purple color with sheer sleeves and a tiny gold belt. She'd paired it with some strappy gold heels that matched the belt. She put on the amber pendant he'd given her and some pearl drop earrings that her dad had given her when she'd turned eighteen. She felt further from her cowgirl self than she ever had before, yet perfectly at home in her skin.

"Damn, you look good," he said.

"Ditto," she said with a wink. "Why do we have a limo?"

"In case things get heated in the car again," he said.

"I assumed when you said you were spending the night that you meant at my place," she said.

"I did," he said. "I just really wanted to shower you with luxury and a limo seemed the right choice. Are you ready to go?"

She nodded. She didn't bother locking her door since the only way on or off the ranch was through the main drive. Will put his hand on the small of her back as they walked to the car. The driver was waiting by the door and he held it open for her. She wasn't sure how to get into the car and still look ladylike.

"Well, you can dress the girl up but that's about it," she said. "How the heck am I supposed to get into the car?"

"You sit down, ma'am, then swing your legs inside," the driver said.

"Thanks," she said. She wasn't embarrassed at having to ask. The truth was if she didn't know how to do something, unless she asked about it, she was never going to learn. She sat down and looked up at

Will as she swung her legs into the car and then she scooted over on the seat and he just smiled at her and then climbed in the way she would have.

"Next time we rent one of these I'm going to insist you wear a kilt so you have to do the same crazy maneuver I had to do," she said.

"Deal," he said.

The driver closed the door and she realized the back of the limo was very intimate. The lighting was low and Will put his arm along the back of the seat and drew her into the curve of his body.

"Thank you for coming out with me tonight," he said.

"Thanks for asking me out. You are spoiling me."

"Figured I had to make up for it since you already know I'm spoiled," he said with a grin that was both cocky and sweet.

"I was just being a bit jealous because I'm one of five and we always had to share everything. You haven't ever really acted spoiled around me," she said.

"Thanks," he said sardonically. The car started moving.

"Where are we going?"

"It's a surprise," he said, taking a silk blindfold from his pocket. "In fact, I'm going to have to insist you put this on."

"Uh, I'm not into any of that kinky *Fifty Shades* stuff," she said. She'd read the books, and while it had been exciting on the page, it wasn't really her thing.

"Understood. This is just to preserve the surprise I have in store for you."

"Okay," she said, turning to allow him to put the blindfold on her.

As soon as he did it, she felt more vulnerable than she would have expected. She reached out to touch him, her hand falling to his thigh. She felt the brush of his breath against her neck and then the warmth of his lips against her skin. She turned her head and felt the line of his jaw against her lips and followed it until their lips met.

Will let her set the pace, which she liked. But then he sucked her lip into his mouth as he rubbed his thumb over the pulse beating at the spot where her neck met her collarbone. She closed her eyes.

The scent of his aftershave and the heat of his body surrounded her.

The limo stopped and Will stopped kissing her.

Damn. He had distracted her. She hadn't been paying attention to anything. Not even how long they'd been in the car.

She reached up to take off the blindfold. "Leave it," he said.

"Will."

"It's part of the surprise," he said. "Trust me?"

Trust him.

She wasn't sure…which was a complete lie. She did trust him or she wouldn't be here. Or maybe it didn't matter if she trusted him or not. She wanted to be here and she was going to do whatever he asked.

Except for the kinky stuff…maybe.

She nodded.

"Good. Now scoot this way," he said, drawing her across the seat. She felt a blast of cold air as the door of the limo was opened and then Will kept his hand on hers, drawing her forward until she was on the edge of the seat.

"Swing your legs around," he said.

She did.

The ground beneath her sandals felt like dirt, not pavement.

"Where are we?"

He didn't answer her question. Instead he lifted her into his arms. "Please come back for us in two hours."

"Yes, sir," the driver said, and Amberley wrapped her arms around Will's shoulders, listening to the sound of the limo driving away.

Then Will started walking and the breeze blew around them a bit chilly until she felt a blast of heat, but they hadn't gone inside. He set her on her feet and took off the blindfold and she saw that they were on a wooden platform with those large infrared heating things positioned around a table. There were twinkle lights strung over the top of the table set for two and covered chafing dishes on a buffet next to it.

The ranch land spread out as far as the eye could see. The sky had started to darken and as she glanced up she saw her angel star.

"Surprised?"

More than he would ever know. It was as if he'd glimpsed into her soul and saw every romantic notion she'd ever had and then amped it up to provide this evening for her. Which meant her heart was in for a whole heap of trouble.

Nine

After almost losing her life at eighteen, Amber had promised herself she was going to live in the moment. And it was something that she'd always strived to do. On the back of a horse it was easy—there was no time to worry about if she was behaving the right way or if someone could see her imperfections. She just hadn't always felt comfortable in her own skin. But tonight she did. In town running errands it was a struggle, which was why she usually had to brace herself before she left her truck and walked among everyone else.

It was easier in Royal because no one knew her history the way folks back in Tyler did. But tonight was one of the few times where she felt totally present and like nothing else mattered.

She faltered a little when she saw the dishes he'd

had made for them. Some of them looked so fancy she was tempted just to stare at them instead of eat them. But Will put her at ease. He was snapping photos and then telling her that he was posting the photos of them online. She figured it was something like the photo story app that Cara had shown her but she wasn't interested.

She didn't want to connect with a world that was bigger than the ranch or Royal and maybe a few folks back in Tyler. That was good enough for her.

Will looked like she imagined a prince would look. He was polished and he talked easily and kept the conversation moving along from topic to topic. He knew horses and led her onto the topic of polo ponies and where she saw the breeding changes leading that field. And it didn't matter that she was dressed like a woman and not a cowgirl—she felt at ease talking about the animals.

"I did read an article last month that talked about a breeding program that a Saudi prince was spearheading. I think it's interesting in that he is working on increasing agility while maintaining stamina."

"That makes sense. I knew a guy in college who had gone to Europe to learn a centuries-old custom of Spanish horse dancing. It is basically training the horse to do very practiced moves, not unlike the Olympic horse events but even more controlled. He used some of those practices when we were playing polo and they worked," Will said.

"There really is room for crossover in all types of training. I was recently trying a technique with Montgomery that I saw used in the Olympics. Barrel racing is speed and mastery not only over the horse, but also over yourself."

"How often do you practice?" he asked.

"I try to get a couple of hours in every day. I am only really participating now when I can get away from the ranch," she said.

"And I couldn't tell the pattern you were using, but is there one? Or do you just have to circle all of the barrels in the least amount of time."

She took a bite of her dinner. "You have to go in a cloverleaf pattern and the one who does it the quickest is named the winner. They use an electric eye to do the timing. The key is to get as close to the barrels as you can so that you are taking the shortest route around them all."

"I'd love to watch you compete sometime," he said.

"Sure. I'll let you know the next time I'm going to a rodeo. I try to stay local here in Texas."

"Cool," he said and she wondered what that meant. Was he going to be in Texas for a while?

It wasn't really a response but she was living in the now. So that meant not pointing out that he could be back in Seattle before her next rodeo. Or would he?

She didn't ask the question because, to be honest, that would make things more complicated. Give her another thing to worry about it and that wasn't what she wanted right now.

"I've never had a guy buy me clothes before. Not even my dad. He used to have my grandma buy us stuff or take us shopping," Amberley said.

"Was it odd? It just reminded me of you," he said.

"Well, you were right. I would never have picked it out. I was surprised when I put it on," she said.

"I'm not surprised, I could picture you in it as soon as I saw it."

"Well, aren't you clever?" she said, winking at him. He was too charming for his own good. She suspected he knew it, as well, because he kept moving through life like nothing could touch him.

She wondered if that was how he had dealt with losing his wife all along or if it was just with her that he ran. Because some of the time he'd seemed to be okay. But then she remembered the other night, when he'd stopped himself from making love to her.

And she wondered if he was pretending like she was. She had gotten pretty damn good at believing the lie she told herself that she was okay. She wanted it to stop being a lie. And she knew she wanted to help Will get to a place where he was okay, too.

She suspected that it would happen in its own time and she knew she had to be patient, but a big part of her was afraid that time was going to take him back to Seattle before she could witness him getting there.

"So there I was standing in the middle of the river in Montana with a client that Dad wanted to impress, and he's asking me where I learned my fly-fishing technique, and all I could think of was if I say the Wii, Dad's never going to forgive me," Will said to Amberley as they finished up their meal. They had been having the most carefree conversation, and Amberley loved how he was telling all these personal stories from his childhood.

"What'd you do? I would have straight up said a video game," she said.

"I said natural instinct," Will said as he took a

sip of his wine. "Then my dad came over and said, 'Yup, that boy has a natural instinct for bull.' The client started laughing and I did, too, and honestly it was one of the first times my dad and I connected."

"That's funny. So did the client do what your dad wanted?" Amberley asked.

"Yes. Dad offered me a job after that, but as much fun as the trip to Montana was I knew that I didn't want to have to work that hard to charm people. Computers are easier," he said. "So I turned down the job and that pissed the old man off but I already had the job offer from Max so he got it."

"What does Max do?" Amberley asked.

"He's an ex-hacker-turned-billionaire tech genius. He owns St. Cloud Security Solutions. I'm the CTO for the company…the Chief Technology Officer."

"Dad would have been happy for me to stay on our ranch," Amberley said. "But I knew if I did then I'd spend the rest of my life there. It would have been easy to hide out there and just keep doing what I'd been doing."

"You wanted more," he said.

"I did. I still do. I like working for Clay and Sophie now that they are a couple, but I really would like to have my own stables someday," she said. If she had one dream it was that. She'd let horses take over the parts that she'd thought she'd fill with kids and a husband.

"Why would you have been hiding out if you had stayed at home?" he asked. "You seem like you grab life by the—I mean, you're pretty gutsy."

She smiled at the way he said that. She had tried grabbing life by the balls, but it had grabbed back, and her father said that actions had consequences, which she'd never gotten until that summer.

She took a deep breath. She'd thought telling Will about the hysterectomy would be the hard part, but this was a big part of who she was and why she was here in Royal.

"Um, well, I… This is sort of a downer, maybe we should save it for another night," she said.

Will nodded. "If that's what you want. But I want to know more about you, Amberley. Not the stuff that everyone can find out. The real you. And I think whatever made you want to hide is probably important."

She pushed her plate forward and folded her arms over each other on the table as she leaned forward. It was cozy and intimate at the table. Will had created an oasis for them in the middle of the Texas night.

"I took a job working at a dude ranch the summer I graduated from high school. I was thinking about what I'd do next and I knew I wasn't going to college. It just wasn't for me."

"Makes sense. You have a lot of natural ability with horses and I read about your rodeo wins online."

"You did?" she asked. "I didn't realize you'd looked me up."

"Yeah. I wanted to know more about you even as I was running from you and pretending that you didn't fascinate me."

"That's corny and sweet," she said.

"Thanks, I think."

Will made her feel like she mattered. It was kind, and it wasn't that others hadn't done that but he made her feel like she mattered to him. That it was personal and intimate and she hadn't had that before.

"So, you're on a dude ranch…"

She sat back in the chair and the words were there in her mind and she practiced them before saying them. It was easy in her head to remember what had happened. The cheap wine they'd bought at the convenience store. The way he'd never driven a pickup truck, so he had convinced her to let him drive. And then when he'd parked it and moved over to make out with her in the front seat until it had gone much farther.

Then of course she'd gotten pregnant and had expected Sam to be, well, a better man than he was. Of course, he'd said he was back to his real life and he'd help her financially but wanted nothing to do with her or the baby. It had hurt and there were times when his rejection haunted her. It made it easier for her to isolate herself on the ranch. But she wasn't going to say any of that to Will.

"There had been a group of guys from back east staying as guests at the ranch. They'd decked themselves out in Western clothes and they were flirty and fun and I ended up hooking with one of them. It was my first time and not his, and I'm afraid that freaked him a little bit and then…" She paused. She wasn't sure she could say the next part.

She looked at Will. He'd stopped eating and was watching her carefully.

She took a deep breath and the words spilled out quickly. Like tearing off a bandage, she did it as fast as she could. "I got pregnant. But there were complications, I started hemorrhaging and I almost died. I did lose the baby, and the only way to save me was for me to have a hysterectomy."

She stopped talking and it felt too quiet. Like even the animals and insects that had been in the background before were surprised by her words. She blinked and realized how much she hated telling this story. She never wanted to do it again.

Will didn't say anything and she started to regret telling him, and then he got up and walked around the table. He pulled her to her feet and into his arms and hugged her close. He didn't say anything to her, just wrapped her in his body, and the panic and the pain that had always been buried with that story started to fade a little bit as he held her and made her feel like she was okay.

That she wasn't damaged and broken.

Will didn't know the words to make everything all right and he could tell by the rusty way the story had come out that she was still a little broken from everything that had happened. He knew because no matter how many firsts he had after Lucy's death there were still things that bothered him. And there was no way that he was ever going to be completely washed clean of the past.

And now he knew that Amberley wasn't going to be, either. She was deeply scarred, as he was.

Hell, he wanted to do something to fix this thing that he couldn't fix.

He thought about how caring about someone could suck sometimes. He'd loved Lucy but had been unable to save her and he was starting to care more deeply for Amberley than he wanted to admit and there was no way in hell he could ever fix what had happened to her. No matter how much he wanted to.

"Siri, play Amberley playlist."

The playlist started and it was Jack Johnson's "Better Together." It was the perfect song for how he felt at this moment. He pulled her into the curve of his body and took one hand in his and kept his other wrapped around her waist as he danced her around the table, singing underneath his breath in that off-key way of his.

"You have a playlist for me?" she asked, tipping her head to the side and resting her cheek against his shoulder.

"I do. It's a bunch of songs that you might not have on vinyl," he said, hoping for a smile. He'd made the playlist this afternoon after she'd left his house. He'd wanted to give her something.

She rewarded him with a little half smile. And then he kept dancing and singing to her. He knew there were some pains that words couldn't heal and that time could only scab over. He had been debating his own pain for a year, trying to figure out if he was going to scar or just have a scab that he kept scratching and refreshing the hurt.

"I like this one," she said.

"I do, too," he said.

He wanted them to be better together. They could bring out the best in each other. Tonight he felt they'd jumped over that first hurdle. But he knew each of them was going to have more obstacles that they would bring to the relationship.

"I think we are going to be more than friends," he said.

"Me, too. I want more than that from you," she said. "But I don't want to make another mistake. I picked a guy who had nothing in common with me before. A man who didn't look at the world the same way I do."

"I care about you, cowgirl," he admitted.

"Me, too, city boy," she said with a grin.

The song changed to "SexyBack" and she just arched one eyebrow at him.

"Oops. Not sure how this got on there," he said.

"Maybe you were thinking about the way our last date ended," she said with a sassy grin.

Music had done what he couldn't as there were sweet and fun songs in the playlist, and after about five songs he noticed she wasn't tense and the tightness around her mouth had faded. She was laughing and smiling and while he still ached for her and the pain she'd gone through, he felt better for having cheered her up.

"So what do you think? Is there a place for the twenty-first-century technology in your music life?" he asked.

"You're a complete goofball, Will. I told you I use the music app on my phone," she said.

"You did but you said it was just for stuff you already loved."

"Not all the songs you selected are newer," she pointed out. "I think you like my kind of music."

"I do like it. And I was trying to ease you into it. Keep the shock value low," he said, aware that they were both talking about something inconsequential to keep from talking about the real emotions that were lying there between them. The truth that was there in the silence under the music that just kept playing on.

"Thank you."

"You're welcome," he said. "How does dessert sound?"

"Sweet?"

Some of her spunk was coming back and that was exactly what he'd been hoping for. "Good, because I asked for pineapple upside-down cheesecake with a salted caramel sauce."

"That sounds interesting," she said.

"Exactly what I was aiming for." He held her chair out for her and she sat back down.

He cleared away the dinner dishes and then brought back dessert. Everything had been set up by a private chef he'd hired in Royal. The dishes had been labeled and set up so that he could easily find them.

"Coffee or an after-dinner drink?" he asked.

"Coffee would be nice," she said.

"Decaf?" he asked.

"God, no," she said.

Another thing they had in common. He poured them each a cup of coffee from the carafe that had been prepared and then took his seat across from her again. He ignored the questions that still rattled around in his head. Instead he looked around at the night sky.

"My app still isn't doing what I want it to, so I'm not sure we are going to see anything fabulous in the sky tonight," Will said. He was unsure how to get the conversation back on track now.

"That's okay. I'm pretty happy sitting here staring at you," she said.

"Yeah?"

"Yup," she said. "Did that thing you did at the club last night work?" she asked.

"I think it might have. Do you know Adam Haskell?"

"Know him personally? No," she said. "But I do know his reputation. He seems to have a gripe about everyone and everything in town. Do you know he gave my riding lessons a low score on Yelp even though he's never taken a class from me?"

"I'm not surprised. He showed up in a relay link that I was chasing and then when I searched on his name it seemed to make sense that he might be the one releasing everyone's secrets. Do you know if he has any computer knowledge?" Will asked. Being able to post a bad review on Yelp and trolling people on social networks didn't take any real knowledge of computers or hacking. And a part of him had thought that Maverick was more skilled than Haskell seemed to be.

Ten

Will was just about to ask Amberley more questions about Haskell when his phone pinged. He ignored it, after making sure it wasn't Erin. Then it pinged again and started ringing.

"Sorry about this but I think I need to take this," Will said.

"Go ahead," Amberley said.

"Brady," he said, answering his phone.

"St. Cloud," Max said. "Where the hell are you? It looks like Haskell might be our man. I need you to come to Royal now. He's leading the cops on a high-speed car chase and I'm with a judge, the sheriff and a lawyer right now getting a warrant to search his property. I need you to analyze what we find and tell me if he's our man."

Will wasn't ready to end his evening with Amberley but business had to come first. This business, any-way. Once Maverick was caught he would be free to focus on Amberley and see where this was leading.

"I'll be there as quickly as I can," he said.

"Good. I'm texting you Haskell's address. Meet me there."

He ended the call and then looked over at Amberley, who was watching him carefully. "Haskell is on the run and Max is getting permission for me to go through his computer. I'm sorry to cut our date short—"

"No, don't be. I want that bastard Maverick caught as much as everyone else in Royal does. What can I do?"

"I could probably use your help going through things at Haskell's if you want to come with me."

"Will the cops let me help?"

"I don't know," he said. "But I didn't want our night to end."

"Me, either. I think I would. I don't really want to go home yet."

"Okay. Let me get the limo and we will head out."

The limo driver was quick to retrieve them and Will had him take them to his car, tipped the driver to move a box from the trunk over to his car while he and Amberley went inside and then sent the driver home. He checked in on Faye and updated Erin on what was happening before he and Amberley drove into town.

"I never imagined your life would be like this. I figured you just did things on your computer and that was it."

Will laughed. "Usually it's not this exciting. In

a big city Haskell could have slipped away anony-mously. And if he was smarter he'd be driving sen-sibly instead of leading the cops on a high-speed chase."

"I know. He's not the brightest bulb according to the gossip I've heard at the diner."

"Really?"

"Yes, why?" she asked.

"It's nothing," he said. But in his mind there was a new wrinkle to Haskell being Maverick. It would take someone really smart to set up the kind of cover that Will had encountered while trolling the web for Maverick's true identity. It seemed a bit far-fetched that someone people considered not so bright would be able to do something like this on his own.

Was he working with someone?

Will was confident he'd be able to find the answers on Haskell's computer.

"Catching cyber criminals isn't usually like this. Though one time I did have to chase a guy down an alleyway. He'd had a program running on the police scanner to alert him if cops were dispatched to his property. It was a clever bit of code," Will said. He'd tried to convince the hacker to give up breaking into secure systems and bring him over to work for him but the guy wasn't interested.

"That must have been... Was it scary? I mean, are hackers and cyber criminals usually armed?"

"Some of them are. But usually I find the evidence and I don't go with the cops to arrest a criminal un-less they are on some sort of mobile relay, where I have to track them while the cops move in. One time I had to wear a bulletproof vest and was stationed in a SWAT truck. There were all these guys with guns and riot gear on and there I was with my laptop...I felt like the biggest nerd."

"You could never be a nerd," she said.

"Thanks. But I can be. I'm sorry our date has taken a crazy turn."

"I'm not. Honestly this is the most exciting thing I've ever done," Amberley said.

He shook his head. There was pure joy in her voice and he realized again how young she was. True, there were only four years between them and she'd had a very harrowing experience when she was eighteen, but the way she was almost clapping her hands together at the thought of being part of the investigation enchanted him. And turned him on.

"Why are you looking at me like that?" she asked.

"Like what?" he countered, trying to sound innocent, not like he'd been imagining her wrapped around him while he kissed her senseless.

"You know," she said.

"Uh, this is the place," Will said as he turned into the driveway of a run-down ranch-style house. The yard was overgrown and there was a big sign that said Keep Off the Grass and No Solicitors.

As they got out of the car, Will noticed there was also a sign in the front window that read Protected by Smith & Wesson.

"Not the friendliest of men," Amberley said. "So what do we do now?"

Max was waiting outside for them and a patrol car was parked at the curb with the lights flashing. Some of the neighbors poked their heads out of the front door but most weren't interested.

"Thanks for coming. The sheriff wants us to help go over the house with his team just to be an extra set of computer expert eyes. He thinks we might see something relevant that his officers would overlook since it's not the kind of crime they are used to dealing with," Max said. "Did I interrupt a date?"

"Yes."

"I'm sorry," Max said. "Dang, I wish this had happened another night."

"Me, too. But it didn't. So let's get this taken care of," Will said.

Max knew that this was the first real date that Will had been on since Lucy's death.

"Do you want to take his computer back to your place?" Max asked.

"Let me see the setup first," Will said. "Do you know Amberley Holbrook? She's the horse master at Clay's ranch."

"Nice to meet you Amberley," Max said.

"Same."

They went into Haskell's house and the cops were gathering other evidence while Max, Will and Amberley found his computer. "This doesn't look very sophisticated."

"No," Will agreed. "It looks like it's about ten years old."

Not that you needed a new or sophisticated machine to hack. Most of the time if he ran from a DOS prompt he could get into over-the-counter software and some social media sites.

Will hit the mouse to see if there had been a program running or if there was a security login.

And then he sat down in the dirty chair to get

to work. He lost himself in the computer programming...or tried to. But the smell of Amberley's perfume lingered in the room and he couldn't help but think this was one time when he didn't want work distracting him from his real life.

Tonight he'd come closer than ever to finding something with Amberley that he hadn't wanted to admit had been missing in his life.

Max and Will talked quietly while the computer ran some program. Everyone had something to do and she was just standing in the corner trying not to get in anyone's way.

She hadn't seen Will work before. She stood there watching him when she thought no one was looking. He was intense as his fingers moved over the keyboard. He took a small dongle from his key ring and plugged it into the USB drive and first lines of text started scrolling on the screen, which meant nothing to her, but Will nodded and then started typing on the keyboard.

"He's one of the best in the world."

She glanced over her shoulder at Max St. Cloud, who stood next to her. She didn't know much about the man except he was Will's partner at St. Cloud Security Systems. She also knew he was engaged to Natalie Valentine, a local wedding dress designer.

"He's awesome," she said, then realized how lame that sounded. "Sorry, I'm really better with horses than people."

Max laughed in a kind way. "It's okay. I should probably leave you alone but I was curious about you."

That didn't sound very reassuring.

"Why?"

"Will hasn't done anything but work since... Faye's birth. I think you're the first woman he's been out with," Max said.

"I know," she said. She was the first. That's why she should be cautious about falling for Will. He was a city guy who'd lost his spouse, so in her mind there were danger signs all around him. But he was also the guy who'd made her a special playlist and could ride like he'd been born in the saddle.

"Good," Max said. "Want to help me look for USB drives, other storage devices, a tablet, maybe an external hard drive?"

"Sure," Amberley said. "I know what some of those things are but what's an external hard drive?"

Max smiled. "Should be a rectangle shape and thin. Follow me, the lead detective needs to give us some gloves and tell us how to search."

Amberley followed him into the other room and after a brief explanation of what they were to do and orders to track down an officer and let him know if they found anything, they were both sent to look.

"If you take the living room and I take the bedroom we might be able to finish this search quickly and get you back on your date," Max said.

"Sounds good," she said.

She followed Max out of the room where Will was working and went into the living room. It was dusty and cluttered, but as Amberley walked around the room she noticed a system. There was a pile of *Royal Gazettes* next to his recliner. The weekly newspaper was stacked up almost to the arm of the chair. She glanced down at the paper on top. It was the one from two weeks ago that had run the story of Will coming to town to help find and stop Maverick.

He'd underlined the word *Maverick*. That was interesting. It could be a clue or maybe Haskell was just ticked off that someone else was ruining the lives of Royal's citizens and taking over his role.

Amberley sorted through the top papers and noticed that he'd used his black pen to mark every story relating to the cyber menace. Was it a kind of trophy for him? Seeing the stories about himself in the paper? She set them in a neat stack on the seat of the chair to show to the officers who were in the house and then started looking through the mess on the side table. There were prescription pill bottles and a community college book on computer software that looked to be about three years old. She stuck that on her pile of stuff and kept moving.

She found some other things that were personal and she realized how odd it was to be going through someone else's house. Haskell always seemed like an old curmudgeon to her when she'd seen him in town but she found a picture of him on one of the bookshelves with a girl from when he'd been in his twenties. He'd been smiling at the camera and he had his arms wrapped around the woman. Amberley didn't recognize her but she wondered what had happened to her.

Was she the reason why Haskell hated the residents of Royal so much now?

"Find anything?" Max asked as he entered the room.

"Not the hard drive, but I did find these papers,

where he has underlined every mention of Maverick. Not really hard evidence but I saw on a crime show that serial criminals like to keep references to their crime as a sort of trophy. So this might mean something. And I found this old computer book on his table. Maybe he was brushing up his skills?" Amberley said. "There's a lot of junk and dust in this room."

"In this house," Max said. "I think the papers might be a lead. And the computer book, let me see that, please."

She handed it to Max. He opened the book and read some of Haskell's handwritten notes. "Let me see if Will can make anything of this."

She followed Max back into the area where Will was. Will turned when they entered.

"He was definitely using an external source," Will told them. "I think if we find that we might find the evidence we need. Did you two find anything?"

"We found this," Max said, handing it over to Will. "It was an MS training class. So not anything in here that would help him mask his online presence. So we're done here?"

"I think so," Will said.

"I'll let everyone know," Max said, leaving the room.

Will went back to the small home office and Amberley followed him, watching from the doorway as he pounded his fists on the desk.

Going in to check on Will hadn't seemed like a bad idea until she put her hands on his shoulders and he pulled her closer to him. He was frustrated—she could see that. He stood up and she looked into his eyes and she wanted to say something or do something to help him not feel so hampered by this investigation.

"Let's finish this up so we can get back to our date," Will said. "I'm not close to being finished with you."

She hoped she looked calmer than she felt because every part of her was on fire and she knew that she'd changed. That sharing the past with Will had freed her in a way she hadn't expected it to.

The secret that she'd always hid from the men she'd hooked up with had been a weight she hadn't even been aware of until now. Until she was free of it. She heard the cops talking and Max went in to talk to Will and she just stood there in the cluttered, dusty living room, knowing that her entire world had changed.

A new hope sprang to life inside her and she wondered if she'd found a man she could trust.

Eleven

"I should get you back home," Will told her as they walked out of Haskell's house.

"Okay," Amberley said, glancing at her watch. "I have to be up early for the horses."

"Wait a second," he said, turning and leaving her by his car to go over to where Max stood.

She watched as he spoke to Max, his business partner and friend, and remembered how Max had talked to her. She wasn't sure if he'd been warning her to be careful with his friend, or just warning her that Will might not be ready for whatever was happening between them.

She rubbed her hand along the back of her neck and shivered a bit. The night was chilly and she was outside without a coat on. But it wasn't too cold. She just suddenly felt very unsure.

And she didn't like it. It wasn't as if Max had said anything that she hadn't been aware of, she knew that Will hadn't dated since Lucy's death. She knew that she might be someone he cared for but she might also be the woman he was using to help him get over losing his wife. But hearing it from someone else's mouth was making her think that maybe she wasn't being smart.

Her heart didn't care and neither did her body. In fact, maybe her being his temporary woman was exactly the right thing for her. He was her first in many ways, too. The first guy she'd told about losing the baby. The first guy she'd really cared about since she was eighteen.

She'd thought she loved Sam. Well…at least cared about him. But this thing she felt for Will was so much stronger. She didn't know if it was real, either. And it was harder than she had anticipated to keep her cool. Not to let her emotions overwhelm her. But when Will came back over, shrugged out of his jacket and draped it over her shoulders, she felt like she was fighting a losing battle inside of herself.

"Max is going to text me if he hears anything," Will said. "Let's go home."

Home.

An image of her, Will and Faye popped into her mind and she didn't want to shove it out. She wanted it to be true. Watching Faye take her first steps today and feeling that punch of joy in her stomach had made her realize that she could have a family. She didn't have to give birth to love a child. And while a part of her realized that it was dangerous to think that way about Will and Faye, another part of her was already putting herself in the picture.

"Okay."

He held open the door for her and she slid into the passenger seat. She slipped her arms into the sleeves of Will's jacket. It smelled like his aftershave and after she fastened her seat belt she put her hands in the pockets and felt something…

She pulled it out. It was a photo. She glanced down at it and saw Lucy. He was carrying around a picture of his wife. The door opened and she shoved the photo back in her pocket, but it caught on the fabric and he noticed her hand as he slid behind the wheel.

"What's that?" he asked.

She felt like there was a weight in the pit of her stomach… "This."

She handed it to him.

He took it and as he did she noticed there was typed information on the back of the photo. And she realized what it was. She had a card like that with her mom's picture on it that she'd gotten at her funeral. It was Lucy's funeral card.

"I—I haven't worn that jacket since the day we buried her," Will said. "I didn't even realize it was in there."

He looked down at the picture and ran his thumb over her features and Amberley felt like she'd interrupted a very private moment. She shouldn't be in the car with him. Or wearing his jacket or even falling for him. She didn't know where Will was in his head but he wasn't with her. Would he ever fully be able to be with her?

That thought hurt more than she'd expected it to.

"She would have liked you," Will said.

"Would she?" Amberley asked.

Watching Will gently caress his late wife's picture gave Amberley an odd feeling. Like when she had cut herself with a knife cooking dinner and she knew she'd cut herself, but it didn't start bleeding right away or hurt for a few seconds. The wound was there. She was just in denial about how deep it went.

"Yes. It's not…I'm not holding on to the past," Will said. "This isn't like the other night."

"Please, you don't have to explain."

"But I want to. Lucy is gone and she's a part of my past," Will said. "She'll always be a part of my life because of Faye."

"I know that. Really I do. I'm not upset," she said. She was trying to make the words true by saying them with conviction but in her heart, she was sad. And she felt just a little bit sorry for herself.

"Amberley."

She looked over at him and she'd never seen him so intense before.

"I want you to know that I'm not dating you just to try to move on from Lucy's death. And I know that we haven't had much time together but I'm not fooling around with you and using you."

She wanted to believe him. He had said the words that she could have asked him to say but she wasn't too sure they were the truth.

Will dropped off Amberley at her place, where she shrugged out of his jacket and gave it back to him. "Thanks for a very interesting date."

"You're welcome," he said. He wanted to come in.

His gut said that he shouldn't just let her walk away, but he didn't know if pushing her now was the right thing to do. So he waited until she was safely inside her house and then drove back to his place.

But when he got there he just sat in the car holding Lucy's picture. Life with Lucy had been uncomplicated. They'd met in college and both of them had come from similar backgrounds. Everyone had said they were a match made in heaven. And while he loved her and cared for her, he knew they'd been growing apart in the months before Faye's birth.

Sometimes he suspected his guilt stemmed from that. That he'd been drifting out of their marriage when she'd died. He went home and the house was quiet with everyone sleeping. He checked in on Faye.

He had the funeral card that Amberley had found earlier and brought it into Faye's room with him. When he looked down at his sleeping daughter's face he could see the resemblance to Lucy. It was growing stronger every day and it made him miss his wife.

He felt a pang in his heart when he thought about raising their daughter alone. And there was a part of him that wondered if he'd ever really be able to bring another woman into their lives. He liked Amberley. He wanted her fiercely but he didn't know if he was right for her.

If she was just a good-time girl, then he wouldn't hesitate to get involved, but everything had changed tonight when she'd told him about the child she'd lost. There was a hidden vulnerability to her that he couldn't ignore now that he'd glimpsed it. And no matter how hot they might burn together he sensed that she was going to want more from him. And he knew she deserved more from him. He couldn't do it.

After a restless night he woke up early and went into the kitchen, where Erin was feeding Faye breakfast. He poured himself a cup of coffee and then sat down.

"How was your date?" Erin asked.

"It was okay. We did get a break in the Maverick case last night."

"That's good," Erin said. "So does that mean we won't be here much longer?"

"I'm not sure yet," Will said. "Why?"

"Just wondering if I should start packing up our stuff. I've got to run a few errands in town this morning," Erin said.

"We'll probably be here at least until the end of the month," he said.

"Okay," she said.

"I'll watch Faye while you go to town," Will said.

"Are you sure?" she asked.

"Yes. I missed spending time with her last night and you had to work overtime."

"You know I don't mind."

Will nodded at her. "I do know that. But I also know errands go quicker without Faye."

"True. Thanks, Will."

"No problem," he said. He moved around to take the spoon from Faye. "Go on. I've got breakfast."

Erin quickly left the room. He touched his daughter's face and she cooed and blinked up at him.

"Hello, angel," he said. "You're hungry this morning."

She kicked her legs and arms and smiled at him. "Dadada."

"That's right. Daddy's here," he said as he scooped her up into his arms.

He held her close and buried his face in the soft curls at the top of her head. He changed her diaper and then carried her into his office. "Ready to help Daddy work?"

"Dadadada," Faye said.

"I'll take that as a yes," he said, then grabbed his laptop and Faye's little toy computer and sat down in the big double chair in the corner. He put his laptop on his lap after he'd set down Faye and she reached for her toy and mimicked his motions.

Then she looked over at him and smiled.

He smiled back at her as she started pounding on the keys with her fingers. His little computer whiz.

He knew he should be looking up some of the information he had found on Haskell's computer, but Amberley was on his mind and he typed her name into the search bar instead. He saw the pictures of her in the rodeo and then did a deeper search and found an old newspaper article from when she was a junior in high school. It was a profile of her as the junior barrel-racing champ with her horse. She looked so young and innocent.

Only seeing that photo of her and comparing it with the woman he knew now showed how much life had changed her. He leaned back and Faye crawled over to him and climbed on his lap the way she did. He lifted her with one hand and shifted his computer out of her way with the other.

She looked at the picture on the screen.

He looked down at her.

"Dadada," she said. Then babbled a string of words that made no sense to him.

Had she recognized Amberley? They'd played together for an entire afternoon but would that be enough for her to recognize her?

And was he doing Faye a disservice by allowing her to get attached to Amberley when Will wasn't sure what was going to happen between them. Sure he'd told her he saw a future with her, but now he was having second thoughts. How could he promise her something like a future when he wasn't even sure where he was going to be in a month's time. He was pretty sure he wasn't going to stay in Royal. His entire family was in Bellevue. His parents and Faye's maternal grandparents. But Lucy's sisters didn't live in Bellevue; one of them was in Oregon and the other in San Francisco.

And after she'd seen that picture of Lucy in his pocket was she going to want to be with him? Did she think he was still hung up on his wife?

Hell.

There were no answers, only more confusion and a little bit of sadness because if there was ever a woman he wanted in his life it was Amberley. She suited him. She wasn't his twin, which was probably why he enjoyed her so much. She was blunt and funny and unafraid to admit when something confused her. She was sassy and spunky and he wanted her to have all the happiness that he saw on her face in that picture when she'd been sixteen.

He didn't want to be the man who'd completed

what the jerk from the dude ranch had started. The man who showed her that she couldn't trust.

But how could he do that for Amberley and not risk hurting himself. He'd promised himself that he would never fall in love again when he'd held Lucy's hand as she lay dying. He'd never felt that abandoned and alone before and he'd promised himself that he'd never feel that way again.

Amberley went about her business all morning, ignoring Will and anyone who wasn't four-legged. Cara arrived on Monday afternoon with the latest news about Adam Haskell. After he'd crashed his car and been captured, an ambulance had transported him to the hospital. Apparently his condition was still critical.

"Sheriff Battle impounded the car. I heard they had to medevac Mr. Haskell to the hospital after he crashed on the highway," Cara said.

"Sounds like it was nuts," Amberley said.

That meant that Will was probably going to be done here in Royal. Everyone seemed to agree that Haskell was Maverick and she was afraid that Will was going to leave now. It hardly mattered that she was still upset with him for the way their date had ended and angry at herself for letting pride make her send him away. But she was tired of trying to compete against a ghost for him.

But she couldn't change the past. She knew that better than anyone.

"Why do you think they were after Haskell? Maybe they finally got tired of his crappy online reviews."

Amberley glanced over at Cara, who was smiling and texting while she was talking to her. "What do you know about Haskell?" Amberley asked. Cara's family had lived in Royal for generations.

Cara looked up from her phone at Amberley. "Not much. He really didn't like high school kids. One time I tried to sell him a magazine subscription and he was a jerk."

"Why did you even bother?"

"Someone dared me," Cara said.

They worked in silence for twenty minutes until they were done with the horses, and Amberley wanted to pretend she'd found some inner peace about Will, but she hadn't.

"Amberley?"

"Yes."

"Will you watch me run the barrels? I need to gain a second or two and I can't figure out where," Cara said.

"Sure. The barrels are set up. I'll go and walk the path while you saddle up." Amberley walked out of the barn and over to the ring to double-check that everything was where it should be.

She noticed that Erin was walking toward the stables with Faye in her arms. The little girl was wearing a pair of denim overalls and a rust-colored long-sleeved shirt underneath it.

"Hi, Erin," Amberley said as the other woman came over to her. Faye held her hands out toward Amberley and she reached over to let her grab on to her finger as the baby babbled at her.

"Hiya," Erin said. "We were out for our afternoon

walk and I thought she might like to see some of the horses."

"Perfect. Cara is going to be out in a minute with her horse to practice. That will be fun to watch."

Amberley couldn't help thinking that Erin was here for something other than to watch the horses. And when Cara came out and noticed they had company, she gave Amberley a look.

"Warm up, Cara. Then let me know when you're ready to take your run," she said. She had a stopwatch on her phone that she'd use to time Cara after she warmed up.

"I didn't realize you were working," Erin said.

"It's okay. You haven't been over to the stables to ride. Do you like horses?" Amberley asked.

"I don't know. I mean, I read books with horses in them growing up but I've never been on one," Erin said.

"We can fix that. Do you want to go for a ride?" she asked.

"Yeah. Sort of. I'm not sure when, though," Erin said.

"Well, the best way to get to know horses is grooming them. And I think even little Miss Faye would like to be in the stables. When Cara is done with her run we could go and meet the horses," Amberley said.

"I'd like that," Erin said.

Faye squirmed around and reached for Amberley. Erin arched an eyebrow at her and held Faye out toward her. Amberley took the little girl in her arms and hugged her. She was going to miss Faye when she and Will left. And though she hadn't spent that much time with the baby she knew she'd become attached to her.

Not her smartest move.

But then everything about Will Brady rattled her.

Cara rode over to the fence and smiled down at Faye.

"Who is this little cutie?"

"Faye Brady. Will's daughter," Amberley said.

"She's adorable," Cara said.

Amberley agreed and she realized that she wanted this little girl to be hers. She wanted that image of the family that had popped into her head last night to be real and she knew it couldn't be. Finding Haskell meant Will would be leaving. Maverick was done terrorizing Royal and Will Brady was going to be leaving Texas and taking a piece of her heart with him.

She handed Faye back to Erin as Cara started doing her run. And Amberley tried to settle up with the fact that this was her life.

Twelve

Sheriff Battle, Will was told, had found a hard drive and some other incriminating evidence in Haskell's car. The police had brought it over to him this afternoon and Will was trying to break the security code to access the info within. The coding was different from anything he'd found on Haskell's home computer. It was more complex and nuanced than what he'd seen before.

Will was on the fence as to whether the same programmer could be responsible for both codes. Haskell had used a complex passcode on his computer, but the security on the hard drive was different. Will used all the skills he'd developed as a hacker back in his teenage days, before he'd settled down to working on the right side of the law.

He kept Max and the sheriff up-to-date on his

progress and after spending six hours working at a cramped desk, he got into the hard drive and found all of the files that Maverick had used to blackmail and scandalize Royal.

"This is it," Will said, calling over the sheriff. "All the files and the paths he used to upload the information are on here. This is pretty much your smoking gun."

"Just what I wanted to hear," Sheriff Battle said. He pulled his cell phone from his pocket. "I'm going to call the hospital and see if he's awake for questioning. Wonder if he has asked for a lawyer yet? Thanks for your help, Will."

"No problem, Sheriff," Will said.

The sheriff turned away and Will heard him ask for Dr. Lucas Wakefield. Will's own phone pinged and he saw that he had a text from Max, who was coming into the building. He went to meet him in the hallway.

"The hard drive had all the evidence the sheriff needs to charge Haskell. He's on the phone to the hospital right now to see if Haskell can be questioned. I'm a little concerned that the coding and some of the scripts on the hard drive were way too sophisticated compared to the home computer, but maybe he was just trying to cover his trail," Will said. "I'll put together some questions about that for the sheriff to ask when they interrogate Haskell."

"There won't be an interrogation," Sheriff Battle said as he came into the hallway. Will and Max turned to face him. "Haskell is dead."

The crash had involved Haskell's car flipping over when he hit a guard rail on the highway. They'd had to use the jaws of life to get him out of the car and then he'd been medevaced to the hospital.

"Well, hell," Will said. He didn't like the lack of closure on this case. He was used to catching hackers and seeing them brought to justice. The entire thing with Haskell was making the back of his neck itch. Something wasn't right. It had been too easy to find the hard drive in his vehicle. Though to be fair, Haskell probably hadn't expected to crash his car and die.

Max had some stronger expletives and the sheriff looked none too happy, either. Will didn't know about the other two but he was beyond ticked off. Hacking was one thing and unmasking cyberbullies was something that he was known for. It frustrated him that he was having such a difficult time unmasking Maverick. And it ticked him off even more to think that the man who'd had the messy house and seemed to have only taken a computer class at the community college had outsmarted everyone in Royal for months before he was fatally injured in a car crash.

Things weren't adding up as far as Will was concerned.

"What were you saying about maybe there being more than one person involved?" Sheriff Battle asked Will.

"It was just a theory. I can't confirm it without information from Haskell. He might have been smarter than everyone thought and used the town's perception of him as cover," Will said.

"Do you feel confident that I can tell the townspeople that Haskell was Maverick?" the sheriff asked him.

No. He didn't. And that wasn't like him. Had he let Amberley distract him from his job? Had he missed something obvious that he shouldn't have? He couldn't say and both men were looking at him for an answer. "The hard drive belonged to Maverick," Will said. "That is definite. But there is no real proof that it was Haskell's or that he programmed it."

"That's not good enough," the sheriff said.

"You could announce that Maverick's been caught and see what happens," Max suggested.

"I'm still running that program from the club's server and I can use the code on the hard drive to start a trace back…to see if I can tie the code to any known hackers on the dark web," Will said.

"Okay. Let's do it. I'm going to hold a press conference and say that we believe Haskell was Maverick. If there are no more attacks then… Hell, this isn't the way I like to do a job. It's half guesswork," Sheriff Battle said.

"I wish we had more to go on but without talking to Haskell there's just not enough on the drive or his personal computer to tie the two together," Will said.

He didn't like it. It felt to him like there was something more going on here.

"Well, I guess we're going to have to play the cards we've been dealt," the sheriff said.

"It could be a group effort," Will said. "In which case exposing Haskell might convince the other members or his partner to go underground."

The sheriff went out to make his announcement and Max took one look at Will and said, "Let's go get a drink."

The two of them went over to the Texas Cattleman's Club, and about thirty-five minutes later the television over the bar was carrying the press conference announcing that Maverick had been identified. A lot of people in the club were surprised but not overly so.

"He always had a beef with the townsfolk of Royal," someone remarked.

"Guess it was his way of getting back at all those supposed slights."

Max took a swallow of his scotch and Will did the same. He couldn't shake the feeling that something wasn't right. Chelsea Hunt joined them a few minutes later.

Will only had to glance at her to know she didn't believe that the trouble with Maverick was over, either. "Scotch?"

"Yes," Chelsea said as she sat down next to Max. "The sheriff brought me up to speed before he started his press conference."

"This isn't the way I expected this to end," Max said.

"Something tells me this isn't over," Will said. "It just doesn't feel like it."

And he was right.

He got a text three hours later when he was halfway back to the ranch that nude pictures of Chelsea Hunt had shown up on the website Skinterest.

The release of the photos seemed to be timed to embarrass the sheriff's department. Will pulled the car over to call Max; he didn't know Chelsea well enough to call her.

"St. Cloud," Max said.

"It's Will. I'm not back at my computer yet but I wanted to let you know that I can run a trace to see if the posting of the nude photos was time delayed or if they were put up after the sheriff's news conference."

"Good. This has gotten out of hand," Max said. "Chels is beyond ticked off. We need to know if it was Haskell."

"I'll do what I can. I'll be in touch soon," he said, hanging up.

The culprit had identified himself as Maverick and there was no doubt in anyone's mind that he was to blame since the way the photos were released was similar to the other scandals Maverick had caused. And after all, Chelsea was the one who'd been spearheading the effort to stop Maverick and she and Max were old buddies, which was how Will and Max had ended up in Royal.

Will remotely started the trace from the Skinterest site and then texted Max back that he should have something in a few hours. He was pissed. It felt like Maverick was thumbing his nose at them. He'd waited until after Sheriff Battle's press conference and, of course, the news that Adam Haskell had died in the hospital. It wasn't that the track was cold; they still had a few leads, but it was damn sure not as hot as it once had been.

Max told him to take the afternoon and evening off and they'd regroup tomorrow to figure out what to do next.

Next?

Will didn't bother to text Max back after that, he just got back on the road. He knew where he needed to be now and it wasn't the guest house he'd called home these last few weeks.

It didn't even matter to him that the way he'd left things with Amberley was less than ideal. He needed her. Needed to see her.

She was another loose end here in Royal and he was tired of running. Tired of feeling like he was losing. He needed to talk to her and…well, more. But he didn't dwell on these things as he pulled up in front of her house.

He sat in the car for a good ten minutes, debating between going up to her door and going somewhere else.

Maybe he would be better suited going to town and finding a rowdy bar and drinking and maybe getting into a fight to work out his frustration. But then her front door opened and she leaned there against the doorjamb wearing a pair of faded jeans and a top that hugged her curves. Her hair was pulled back in its customary braid.

She chewed her lower lip as their eyes met.

He turned off his car, shutting off the sound of screaming death metal that he'd put on because it suited his mood, and got out.

"We lost Maverick. It wasn't Haskell."

"I heard the news," she said. "Cara was texting with one of her friends in town when the Skinterest link popped up."

"I'm so…I don't know why I came here. I'm frustrated and edgy and I just couldn't go home and the only place I want to be is with you."

She nodded. "Then come on in."

He crossed her yard in angry steps and climbed

up the stairs. She stepped back to give him room to walk past her. But as soon as he stepped inside and smelled the fragrance of apples and cinnamon, his temper started to calm.

"I've got whiskey or beer, if you want to drink. I've got a deck of cards if you want to play poker. I would say we could go for a ride but I'm not a big fan of riding when you're upset. I think it puts the horse in danger," she said.

"I don't want to ride horses," he said.

"Good. So what's it going to be? Did I list anything that sounds good to you?" she asked.

"No," he said. "I want you. I can't think of anything except your mouth under mine and my body inside yours."

She flushed but didn't move from where she stood with her back against the cream-colored wall. Then, with a nudge of her toe, she pushed the front door. It closed with a thud and she stepped away from the wall.

"Where do you want me?" she asked.

"Are you sure?" he asked. Because even as he was walking toward her, his blood running heavy in his veins, he wanted to give her a chance to say no.

"Yes. Make that a 'hell, yes.' I have been aching for you, Will. Every night when I go to bed I'm flooded with fantasies of you and me together. That orgasm you gave me was nice but it only whetted my appetite and left me hungry for more."

"I'm hungry, too," he said.

Will walked forward until not even an inch of space separated them. He pulled her into his arms, kissing her slowly, thoroughly and very deeply. He caught her earlobe between his teeth and breathed into her ear, then said, "I'm not sure how long I can last."

She shivered delicately, her hands clutching his shoulders, before she stepped back half an inch.

"That's okay," she said, and it was. She had been dreaming of this moment—when he would forget about everything except her, when he needed her more than anything else. She wasn't about to let him slip away again without knowing what it was like to make love to him.

She tugged the hem of her thermal shirt higher, drawing it up her body, and he touched her stomach. His hands were big and warm, rubbing over her as she pulled the shirt up and over her head. She tossed it on the floor and he put his hands on her waist, turning her to face the mirror in the hallway.

He undid the button of her jeans and then slowly lowered the zipper. She stared at them in the hall mirror, concentrating on his hands moving over her body. Then, she glanced up to see he was watching her in the mirror, as well.

Their eyes met and he brought his mouth to her ear, and whispered directly into it, "I love the way you look in my arms."

He stepped back, tugged at her jeans and then slid them down her legs. She shimmied out of them, leaving her clad in only a pair of whisper-thin white cotton panties. Delicately she stepped out of the jeans pooled at her ankles, balancing herself by putting one hand on the table in front of her.

The movement thrust her breasts forward. He unclasped her bra, her breasts falling free into his wait-ing hands. She looked in the mirror as a pulse of pure desire went through her. He stood behind her, his erection nestled into the small of her back. His hands cupped her breasts, and his eyes never left her body as his fingers swirled around her nipples.

She turned in his arms, reaching up to pull his head down to hers. Her mouth opened under his and she wanted to take it slow but she couldn't. She was on fire for him. He was everything she ever wanted in a man and he was here in her arms.

He slid his hands down her back and grasped her buttocks, pulling her forward until he could rub the crown of his erection against her center. She felt the thick ridge of his shaft against her through the fab-ric of his pants. He reached between them to caress her between her legs.

He lowered his head, using his teeth to delicately hold her nipple while he flicked it with his tongue, and she moaned his name. She brought her hands up to his hair and held his head to her. He lifted his head and blew against her skin. Her nipples stood out. He ran the tip of one finger around her aroused flesh. She trembled in his arms.

Lowering his head, he took the other nipple in his mouth and suckled her. She held him to her with a strength that surprised her. She never wanted to let him go.

Her fingers drifted down his back and then slid around front to work on the buttons of his shirt. She pushed his shirt open. He growled deep in his throat when she leaned forward to brush kisses against his chest.

He pulled her to him and lifted her slightly so that her nipples brushed his chest. Holding her carefully, he rotated his shoulders and rubbed against her. Blood roared in her ears. She reached for his erection as he shoved her panties down her legs. He was so hard as she stroked him. She needed him inside her body.

He caressed her thighs. She moaned as he neared her center and then sighed when he brushed his fingertips across the entrance to her body.

He slipped one finger into her and hesitated for a second, looking down into her eyes. She didn't want his fingers in her, she wanted him. She bit down on her lower lip and with minute movements of her hips tried to move his touch where she needed it. But then she realized what she was doing and reached between them, tugging on his wrist.

"What?"

"I want you inside me," she said. Her words were raw and blunt and she felt the shudder that went through him.

He plunged two fingers into her humid body. She squirmed against him. "I will be."

"I need you now."

He set her on her feet and turned her to face the mirror.

"What are you doing?" she asked, looking over her shoulder at him.

"I want you to watch us as I make love to you. Bend forward slightly."

She did as he asked. Her eyes watched his in the mirror. "Take your shirt off, please. I want to see your chest."

He smiled at her as he finished taking off the shirt

she'd unbuttoned. His tie was tangled in the collar but he managed to get them both off. He leaned over her, covering her body with his larger one.

He bent his legs and rubbed himself at the entrance of her body. She pushed back against him but he didn't enter her. He was teasing her and she was about to burn up in his arms.

"Will."

"Just a second," he said. "Keep your eyes on mine in the mirror."

"Yes," she said, meeting his forest green gaze with her own.

He bit down on her shoulder and then he cupped both of her breasts in his hands, plucking at her aroused nipples. He slipped one hand down her body, parting her intimate flesh before he adjusted his stance. Bending his knees and positioning himself, he entered her with one long, hard stroke.

She moaned his name and her head fell forward, leaving the curve of her neck open and vulnerable to him. He bit softly at her neck and she felt the reaction all the way to her toes when she squirmed in his arms and thrust her hips back toward him, wanting to take him deeper.

He caressed her stomach and her breasts. Whispered erotic words of praise in her ears.

She moved more frantically in his arms, her climax so close and getting closer each time he drove deep. His breath brushed over her neck and shoulder as he started to move faster, more frantically, pounding deep into her.

He slid one hand down her abdomen, through the slick folds of her sex. Finding her center. He stroked the aroused flesh with an up-and-down movement that felt exquisite and drove her closer and closer to her climax.

He circled that aroused bit of flesh between her legs with his forefinger then scraped it very carefully with his nail. She screamed his name and tightened around his shaft. Will pulled one hand from her body and locked his fingers on hers on the hall table. Then penetrated her as deeply as he could. Biting down on the back of her neck, he came long and hard.

Their eyes met in the mirror and she knew that she wasn't falling for him. She'd fallen. She wanted this man with more than her body. She wanted him with her heart and with her soul.

Thirteen

Will lifted Amberley into his arms and carried her into the living room. She had deserved romance and a night to remember and he'd given her sex. He wanted it to be more. Because she was more than a hookup to him.

"Are you feeling relaxed now?" she asked with a grin.

"I'm definitely calmer than I was when I arrived," he said, pulling her onto his lap and holding her closer. "I'm sorry if I was too—"

"You were fine. We both needed that. For the first time I feel like you let your guard down around me," she said.

He had.

He shouldn't have because that meant he was letting her in and he wasn't sure there was room in the gray and gloomy parts of his soul. He had been too good at keeping everyone at arm's length. And now he was unsure what would come next.

"Want to talk about it?" she asked.

"No."

"Sorry. I thought maybe if you talked about what Maverick was doing I could help. Offer some insights."

Of course.

Maverick.

She hadn't read his mind and seen the tortured way he was trying to figure out how to hold on to her and not let go of Lucy. He had to get past that. This was the first time he'd made love to a woman since his wife's death. Maybe the second time like their second date would help him move forward.

"I hadn't thought of it that way," he said.

"I'm not sure why I offered to talk except that I'm nervous. I don't know what to do now."

"What do you usually do?" he asked.

She flushed. "I don't have a habit. I'm still new to this."

"Oh…" That was telling. She'd never trusted a man enough to have him in her house.

And here he was.

"Okay, well, do you want me to leave?" he asked.

"No. Will, you are the one guy that I really want to stay. I need you here."

She needed him.

Those words warmed his heart and made him feel invincible. Like he would do anything for her.

He knew that feeling.

He was falling in love with her.

His heart, which he'd thought was down for the count, was beating again and beating for this woman.

"How about if you go get a shower while I set up a little surprise for you in the bedroom."

"What kind of surprise? I thought you came here without thinking about it?"

"Enough with the questions, cowgirl, it's a yes or no, that's it."

"Yes."

"Stay in the bathroom until I come and get you," he said.

"I will."

She walked away and he watched her leave. He wanted to make sure he committed as much of Amberley to memory as he could. He stayed there on the couch for another minute then stood, fastened his jeans and put on his shirt.

He saw her jeans, shirt and underwear strewn in the hallway and remembered the animalistic passion that had taken over him.

Maybe that was what it had taken to break through the icy wall he'd put around his heart. But there was no going back now.

He folded her clothes and set them on the table by the door and then went out to his car and opened the trunk, where he had placed the box from their romantic dinner. The box he was supposed to have put to good use then. Well, now was definitely the right time.

He opened the box and took out the CD he'd made for her. She liked old-school stuff and he thought the music mix he'd burned onto it would be a nice surprise for her the next time she got in her truck.

He opened the door to the cab, which she never kept locked, pulled down the visor and grabbed the keys. He turned the key to the accessory position and ejected the CD she had in there. Garth Brooks.

He wasn't surprised. He pushed in the CD he'd made for her and then shut off the truck and got out after putting the keys back up in the visor.

He reentered the house and heard her singing in the shower and smiled to himself.

He wanted this night to be perfect. He wanted to give her a gift that was equal to what she'd given him when she'd welcomed him into her life and her body.

Luckily the flowers he'd had in the box were still somewhat preserved and he took his time placing rose petals in a path from the bathroom door leading to the bed. Then he strewed them on the bed. Next he took the candles out of the box and put them on different surfaces. They were fragrant lavender and he lit them before stepping back to admire his handiwork.

He heard the shower shut off. But he wasn't ready yet. He took one of the low wattage Wi-Fi stereo bulbs that he'd placed in the box and installed it in the lamp next to her bed.

Then he cued up his "Amberley" playlist and connected his iPhone wirelessly to the lightbulb. He hit Play and went to the bathroom door, realizing he was overdressed for this. He took off his clothes, neatly folding them on the comfy chair in the corner of the room.

"Will? Are you out there?"

"I am. Stay there," he ordered.

He walked over to the bathroom and opened the

door, quickly stepping inside so he wouldn't ruin the surprise that waited for her.

He washed up quickly at the sink while she combed her hair. "I need you to close your eyes."

"I'm still not—"

"Into the kinky stuff. I know," he said with a laugh.

She made him happy. And he hadn't realized what a gift joy was until he'd spent so long without it in his life.

"Can I open my eyes now?" she asked.

"Yes."

She wasn't sure what she'd been expecting but this was the perfect romantic fantasy. There were rose petals under her feet, candles burning around the room and soft, sensual music playing.

Will put his hands on her shoulders and guided her to the bed.

"Surprised?"

"Yes!"

She turned in his arms and he took her mouth in his, letting his hands wander over her body, still amazed that she was here in his arms.

She buried her red face against his chest. "I wasn't sure if I would see you again or if you were going to leave and go back to Bellevue without saying goodbye."

Her words hurt him but he couldn't argue with them. He hated that he'd done this to her. That his own grief and doubts had been transferred to her.

"I promise I would never leave without saying goodbye," he said. Then to distract her, he picked up a handful of the rose petals that littered the bed and, turning her onto her back, he dropped them over her breasts.

She shivered and her nipples tightened. He arranged the petals on each of her breasts so that her nipples were surrounded by the soft rose petals. "I'm not surprised. You're a noticing kind of guy."

He leaned down to lick each nipple until it tightened. Then he blew gently on the tips. She raked her nails down his back.

"Are you listening to me?" she demanded.

He made a murmuring sound, unable to tear his gaze from her body. He'd never get enough of looking at her or touching her—he was starting to fall for her and that felt like a betrayal. Something he wouldn't let himself think about tonight.

"I'm listening to your body," he said, gathering more rose petals. He shifted farther down her body and dropped some on her stomach.

Her hand covered his. She leaned up, displacing the petals on her breasts. She took the petals on her stomach and moved them around until they formed a circle around her belly button.

He did just that, taking his time to fix the petals and draw her nipples out by suckling them. He moved the petals on her stomach, nibbling at each inch of skin underneath before replacing the rose petals. Then he kneeled between her thighs and looked down at her.

He picked up another handful of petals and dropped them over the red hair between her legs. She swallowed, her hands shifting on the bed next to her hips.

"Open yourself for me," he said.

Her legs moved but he took her hands in his, bringing them to her mound. She hesitated but then she pulled those lower lips apart. The pink of her flesh looked so delicate and soft with the red rose petals around it.

"Hold still," he said.

He arranged the petals so that her delicate feminine flesh was the center. He leaned down, blowing lightly on her before tonguing that soft flesh. She lifted her hips toward his mouth.

He drew her flesh into his mouth, sucking carefully on her. He crushed more petals in both of his fists and drew them up her thighs, rubbing the petals into her skin, pushing her legs farther apart until he could reach her dewy core. He pushed his finger into her body and drew out some of her moisture, then lifted his head and looked up her body.

Her eyes were closed, her head tipped back, her shoulders arched, throwing her breasts forward with their berry hard tips, begging for more attention. Her entire body was a creamy delight accented by the bloodred petals.

He lowered his head again, hungry for more of her. He feasted on her body the way a starving man would. He brought her to the brink of climax but held her there, wanting to draw out the moment of completion until she was begging him for it.

Her hands left her body, grasped his head as she thrust her hips up toward his face. But he pulled back so that she didn't get the contact she craved.

"Will, please."

He scraped his teeth over her clitoris and she screamed as her orgasm rocked through her body.

He kept his mouth on her until her body stopped shuddering and then slid up her.

"Your turn," she said, pushing him over onto his back.

She took his erection in her hand and he felt a drop of pre-cum at the head. She leaned down to lick it off him. Then took a handful of the rose petals and rubbed them up and down his penis.

She followed her hand with her tongue, teasing him with quick licks and light touches. She massaged the petals against his sac and then pressed a few more even lower. Her mouth encircled the tip of him and she began to suck.

He arched on the bed, thrusting up into her before he realized what he was doing. He pulled her from his body, wanting to be inside her when he came. Not in her mouth.

He pulled her up his body until she straddled his hips. Then using his grip on her hips, he pulled her down while he pushed his erection into her body.

He thrust harder and harder, trying to get deeper. He pulled her legs forward, forcing them farther apart until she settled even closer to him.

He slid deeper into her. She arched her back, reaching up to entwine her arms around his shoulders. He thrust harder and felt every nerve in his body tensing. Reaching between their bodies, he touched her between her legs until he felt her body start to tighten around him.

He came in a rush, continuing to thrust into her until his body was drained. He then collapsed on the bed, laying his head between her breasts. He didn't want to let her go. But he wasn't sure he deserved to keep her.

* * *

I would never leave without saying goodbye.

The words suddenly popped into her head as Will got up to grab them both some water from the kitchen.

He'd said he wouldn't leave without saying goodbye.

But that meant he was still planning to leave.

She sat up, pulling the blanket with her to cover her nakedness.

He came back in with two bottles of water and a tray of cheese and crackers. "Thought you might want a snack."

"Thanks," she said.

He sat on the edge of the bed and she crossed her legs underneath her. Why had he done all of this? Created the kind of romantic fantasy that made her think…well, that he could love her. And he was only going to leave?

He handed her a bottle of water and she took it, putting it on the nightstand beside her bed.

"Will, can I ask you something?"

"Sure," he said.

"Did you say you won't leave without saying goodbye?"

"Yes. I wouldn't want you to wonder if I'd gone," he said.

"So you are still planning to leave?" she asked.

He twisted to face her.

"Yes. You know my life is back in Bellevue," he said. "I'm just here to do a job."

He was here to do a job.

She'd known that. From the beginning there had

been no-trespassing signs all over him and she'd tried to convince herself that she knew better.

But now she knew she hadn't.

"Then what the hell is all of this?"

He stood up and paced away from the bed over to the chair where his clothes were and pulled on his pants.

"It was romance. The proper ending to our date last night. I wanted to show you how much you mean to me."

She wasn't following the logic of that. "If I mean something to you then why are you planning to leave? Or did you think we'd try long-distance dating?"

"No, I didn't think that. Your life is here, Amberley, I know that. My world... Faye's world is in Bellevue."

"Don't you mean Lucy's world?" she asked. "Faye seems to like Royal pretty well and as she's not even a year old I think that she'd adjust. You said yourself Lucy's parents travel and your folks seem to have the funds to visit you wherever you are."

"It's my world, too," he said. "I care about you, Amberley, more than I expected to care about another woman again, but this...isn't what I expected. I made a promise to myself that I'd never let another woman into my life the way I did with Lucy. Losing her broke me. It was only Faye and friends like Max that kept me from disappearing. And I can't do that again."

She wasn't sure why not. "I'm willing to risk everything for you."

She watched his face. It was a kaleidoscope of emotions and, for a brief moment, as his mouth softened into that gentle smile of his, she thought she'd gotten through to him.

"I'm not. It's not just myself I have to think of. It's Faye, as well," he said. "And it's not fair to you to put you through that. You've lost enough."

"Lost enough? Will, I think…I think I love you. I don't want to lose you," she said. "If you asked me to go with you to Bellevue, I would." She knew she was leaving herself completely open but she had lost a lot in her young life. First her mom, then her innocence and then her baby. And she'd thought she'd stay locked away for the rest of her life but Will had brought her back to the land of the living.

If she didn't ride all out trying to win him over, then she would be living with regret for the rest of her life.

"You would?" he asked.

"Yes. That's what you do when you love someone."

Saying she loved him was getting easier. She got up from the bed and walked over to him. She put her hand on his chest and looked up into his eyes.

"I know your heart was broken and battered when Lucy died. I know that you are afraid to risk it again. But I think we can have a wonderful life together. I just need to know that you're the kind of man who will stand by my side and not turn tail and run."

He put his hand over hers and didn't say a word. He lowered his head and kissed her, slowly, deeply, and she felt like she'd gotten through to him. Like she'd finally broken the wall around his heart.

He lifted her in his arms and carried her back to the bed. "Will?"

Instead of answering he kissed her. The kiss was

long and deep and she felt like it was never going to end. And it didn't end until he'd made love to her again.

She wanted to talk. It felt like they needed to but he pulled her closer to him and she started to drift off to sleep in his arms. His hand was so soothing, rubbing up and down her back, and she wondered if words were really needed. She'd finally found the life she'd always wanted in the arms of the man she loved.

When she woke in the morning she sat up and realized she was alone in bed.

"Will?"

She got up and walked through the house but it was almost silent. She had always liked this time of the morning. She wondered if Will would like to take a morning ride. She wanted to show him the south pasture.

The clock echoed through the house and she realized it was very quiet.

Too quiet.

It was empty except for her.

He hadn't made love to her last night. It hadn't been the joining of two hearts that she'd thought it was. That had been his way of saying goodbye.

Tears burned her eyes and she sank down on the floor, pulling her knees to her chest and pressing her head against them. Why was she so unlovable? What was it about her that made men leave? And why couldn't she find a man who was as honorable as she believed him to be?

Fourteen

Amberley had thought she was ready for whatever happened with Will, but waking up alone... She should have expected it, but she hadn't and she was tired. She called Clay's house and asked for some time off. He wasn't too pleased to be down a person right around the big Halloween festival they were hosting this coming weekend and she promised she was just taking a quick trip home and she'd be back for that.

But there were times when a girl needed to be home. She wanted to see her brothers and sisters and just be Amberley, not the complicated mess she'd become since that city slicker had come into her life with his spiked hair and tight jeans. He'd looked at her with those hungry eyes and then left her wanting more.

Enough.

She wasn't going to find answers in her own head. She needed space and she needed to stop focusing on Will Brady. He had left. He'd said goodbye in a way she'd never really expected him to.

She got Montgomery into his horse trailer and then hit the road. She wasn't going to even glance at the guest house where Will and Faye were staying, but she couldn't help her eyes drifting that way as she pulled by his place. His car was in the drive, like that mattered. He wasn't in the right frame of mind to be her man. In a way she guessed he was still Lucy's.

She tried to tell herself she hadn't been a fool again but the truth was she felt like an idiot. What a way to be starting a long drive. She hit a button on the radio and the CD she had cued up wasn't one she'd put in there. She ejected it and read the Sharpie-written label.

Old-School Mix Tape For My Cowgirl.

She felt tears sting the backs of her eyes.

God, why did he do this? Something so sweet and simple that could make her believe that there was more between the two of them than she knew there was. She'd given him three chances and each time he'd wormed his way even deeper into her heart. And yet she was still sitting here by herself.

She couldn't resist it and finally put the CD back into the player and the first song that came on was "SexyBack."

She started to laugh and then it turned to tears.

He'd set the bar pretty high and it left both of them

room to fall. He'd made her expect things from him that she'd never thought she'd find with anyone else.

She hit the forward button and it jumped to the next track. That Jack Johnson song that he'd danced with her to. The one that had cured her broken heart and her battered inner woman who'd felt broken because she couldn't have her own child. He'd danced with her and made that all okay.

And maybe…

Maybe what?

"Hell, you're an idiot, Amberley. You used to be smart but now you are one big fat dummy. He's messed up."

But she knew that wasn't true or fair. He was broken, too. And she'd thought they were falling in love, that they would be able to cure each other, but instead…they were both even more battered than before. She should have known better.

Her and city guys didn't mix. Did she need some big-ass neon sign to spell it out?

She had no idea as the miles passed but the flat Texas landscape dotted with old oil derricks changed to the greener pastures of the hill country and she just kept driving. She'd expected the pain of leaving to lessen the farther she got from the Flying E ranch but it didn't. So when she stopped to let Montgomery out of the trailer and give him some water, she couldn't help herself. She wrapped her arms around her horse's neck and allowed herself to cry. Montgomery just neighed and rubbed his head against hers.

She put him back in the trailer, wiped her eyes and got back on the road again, pulling onto the dirt road that led to her family ranch just after sunset. She pulled over before she got to the house, putting her head on the steering wheel.

"God, please let me fall out of love with him," she said.

She put the truck back in gear and drove up to the old ranch house where she'd grown up, and the comfort she'd wanted to find there was waiting.

Her siblings all ran out to meet her. Her brothers took Montgomery to the stables while her sisters dragged her into the kitchen to help them finish baking cookies. They chatted around her and the ache in her heart grew. She knew she'd wanted this kind of family for herself and while it was true Will wasn't the last man on the planet, he'd touched her deep in her soul.

She'd started dreaming again about her future, had allowed herself to hope that she could have a family like this of her own, and now it was gone.

It was going to take a lot for her to trust a man enough to want to dream about sharing her life with him. And she was pretty damn sure she wasn't going to be able to love again.

He dad came in and didn't seem surprised to see her.

"Clay called and said you were heading this way. Everything okay?" he asked.

"Yes. Just missed seeing you all and we always carve pumpkins together," Amberley said.

"Yay. Dad said you might not make it home this year," her sister said. "But we knew you wouldn't disappoint us."

"That's right. Dad just knows how busy life is on

the ranch. I was lucky to get a few days off before the Halloween rodeo we're having on the Flying E."

Her dad nodded but she could tell that he knew she was here for more than a seasonal activity. Her siblings brought out the pumpkins and they all gathered around the table and worked on their masterpieces. She sang along to her dad's old "Monster Mash" album from K-Tel that he'd had as a boy growing up.

Tawny slipped her arms around Amberley as they were each picking a pumpkin to carve. "I'm glad you're home. I missed you."

"I missed you, too," Amberley said. "Daddy sent me a video of your barrel run last weekend. Looking good, little missy."

"Thank you. Randy said one day I might be as fast as you," Tawny said.

Amberley ruffled her fifteen-year-old sister's hair. "I'm guessing you're going to be faster than me one day soon."

"She might," Daddy said. "Randy's got himself a girl."

"Dad."

"Do you?" Amberley asked. "How come that's never come up when you call me?"

"A man's allowed to have some secrets."

"Unless Daddy knows them," Michael said.

"How did Daddy find out?" Randy asked.

"I might have told him that you were sweet on someone in town," Michael said.

Randy lunged toward Michael and the two of them started to scuffle the way they did and Amberley laughed as she went over and pulled Randy off his younger brother. "Want to talk about her?"

"No. Let's carve pumpkins," Randy said.

And they did. Each of them worked on their own gourd, talking and teasing each other. Amberley just absorbed it all. As much as she loved the quiet of her cottage she had missed the noise of family. She felt her heart break just a little bit more. When she was in Will's arms it was easy to tell herself that she could have had this with him. Could have had the family of her own that she'd always craved.

After everyone was done carving they took their jack-o'-lanterns to the front porch and put candles inside them. They then stood back to admire their handiwork. Her dad came over and draped his arm around Amberley's shoulder.

"You okay, girl?" he asked.

"I will be," she said.

"You need to talk?"

"Not yet, Daddy. I just needed some hugs and to remember what family felt like," she said.

Her father didn't say anything else, just drew her close for a big bear hug that made her acknowledge that she was going to be okay. She was a Holbrook and they didn't break…well, not for good.

Her heart was still bruised but being back with her family made her realize that the problem wasn't with her. It was with Will. He'd told her that he was in a world of firsts and she should have given him space, or at the very least tried to protect her heart a little more because he wasn't ready for love. And a part of her realized he might never be.

* * *

Will locked himself away in his office, telling Erin that he couldn't be disturbed. There were no leads on Maverick and that was fine with him. He wasn't in any state of mind to track down a kid who'd hacked his parents' Facebook accounts, much less a cyberbully who was too clever for his own good.

His door opened just as he was reaching for the bottle of scotch he kept in his desk. He was going to get drunk and then in a few days he was going to pack up and go back to Bellevue. But he didn't want to leave Amberley. He wished there was a way to talk to Lucy. To tell her he was sorry for their fighting and that he had never thought he'd find someone to love again. But that he had.

He loved Amberley. He knew that deep in his soul. But he had been too afraid to stay. He realized that losing her the way he'd lost Lucy would break him completely. That he'd never survive that. So instead of staying, he left.

"I said I'm busy."

Will saw his partner standing in the doorway with Chelsea. She looked tougher than the last time he'd seen her and he couldn't say he blamed her. "Come in. Sorry for being so rude a moment ago."

"That's fine," Chelsea said. "I've been biting everyone's heads off, as well. Did you find anything on the remote trace you did?"

Max followed her into his office and they both sat down on the couch against the wall. Will turned back to his computer.

"Yes. The coding was the same as what we recovered on the hard drive and I can tell you that it wasn't a time-delayed post. The person who put the photos up definitely has a Skinterest profile so I have been working on getting into that," Will said. "I should have an answer for you in a few days."

"Thank you," Chelsea said. "I am not above hacking the site if I have to. I'm done playing games with Maverick."

"I think we all are," Will said.

Chelsea's phone went off and she shook her head. "I have to get back to town. Thanks for your help on this project, Will."

"I wish I could have gotten to Haskell before he ran," Will said.

"Me, too," Max said. "Go on without me, Chels. I need to talk to my partner."

She nodded and then left. Max reached over, pushing the door shut.

"Give me everything you have so far," Max said.

"Why?"

"Because I think you have been working this too hard. You need a break."

"Uh, we're partners. I don't work for you," Will said.

"We are also friends. And you need a break," Max said. "I think you've been too busy. I think you should take a break."

Will turned in his chair to look at Max. He didn't want to do this. He needed time before he was going to be anything other than a douche to anyone who spoke to him.

"I can't."

"You can," Max said. "This isn't about Maverick."

"How do you know?"

"Because I saw the way the two of you were the other night," Max said.

"I don't know what you saw," Will said.

"Lying to me is one thing, I just hope you aren't lying to yourself," Max said.

His friend had always had a pretty good bullshit detector. "Hell."

Max laughed and then walked over to Will's desk, looked in the bottom drawer and took out the scotch. "Got any glasses?"

Will opened another drawer and took out two glasses. Max poured them both a generous amount and then went to sit on the chair in the corner where Will and Faye usually sat.

He took a swallow and Will did as well, realizing that Max was waiting for him to talk.

"I—I think I'm in love with her. And I don't know if I should be. What if I let her down? What if I can't be the man she needs me to be."

"Good. It's about time. Lucy wouldn't have wanted you to die when she did."

"But I did, Max. I lost some part of myself when she died that day. It was so unexpected."

"I know. I remember. But time has passed and she'd forgive you for moving on."

"I don't want to forget her," he said after a few minutes had passed. That was his fear along with the one that something would happen to Amberley now that he had let her into his heart, as well.

"You won't. Faye looks like Lucy and as she grows up, she'll remind you of her, I'm sure of that," Max said. "But if you are still punishing yourself you won't see it. All you will ever see is your grief."

Will knew Max was right. "I think I feel guilty that I have this new love in my life. You know Lucy and I were having some problems before...well, before everything. Just fighting about how to raise Faye and if Lucy should quit her job."

"You aren't responsible for her death," Max said. "You were fighting—all couples do that. It had nothing to do with what happened to Lucy."

"Logically I know that. But..." Will looked down in his drink. "It's hard to forgive myself."

"You're the only one who can do that," Max said, finishing his drink. "But I do know that you have to move forward. So that's why I'm going to do you a favor."

"You are?"

"Yup. You are on official leave from St. Cloud."

He leaned forward in his chair. "Are you serious?"

"Sort of. I'm not firing you but I think you need to take some time off. Don't worry about the investigation, we got this without you. You've been working nonstop and grieving and I think it's time you started living again."

"What if she won't take me back?" Will asked his friend.

"If she loves you, she will," Max said.

Max got up to leave a few minutes later and Will said goodbye to his friend, then walked him out. He realized that he'd been stuck in the past because of guilt, but also because of fear. And he wasn't afraid anymore. Amberley had said she loved him, and he'd made love to her and walked away rather than let her see how vulnerable that made him.

And he did love her.

He wanted to make his life with her. He scooped Faye up off the floor where she was playing and swung her around in his arms. His baby girl laughed and Will kissed her on the top of her head.

"Are you okay?" Erin asked.

"I'm better than okay," he said.

In fact he needed to get making plans. He needed to show a certain cowgirl that he wanted to be in her life and that he could fit into it.

He asked Erin to keep an eye on Faye while he went to find Clay Everett. He was going to need some serious lessons in being a Texas man if he was going to win over Amberley. He knew he'd hurt her and he hoped she could forgive him. Because he was determined to spend the rest of his life showing her how wrong he'd been and how much he loved her.

Amberley felt refreshed from her time with her family but she was glad to be back on the Flying E. The time away had given her some perspective. Will was in a tough spot and maybe he'd get past it and come back to her. But if he didn't…well, she knew that she wasn't the kind of woman to give her heart lightly. And she also wasn't the kind of woman to wallow in self-pity. She loved him and though living without him wasn't what she wanted, she'd give him time to realize what he was missing out on.

"Hi, Amberley," Clay called as she walked over to the area where the rodeo was set up on the Flying E. She saw Emily and Tom Knox, who had recently announced they were expecting a baby boy. Brandee Lawless was there taking a break from all the wedding planning she'd been doing and Natalie and Max were hanging together near the bleachers.

They had two rings set up and some bleachers for townsfolk. All of the kids from town were dressed up in their Halloween costumes.

"Hey, Clay. I just finished my shift at the dummy steer booth. The kids love roping those horns mounted in the hay bales. Where do you need me now?" she asked. She might have decided that she could give Will time, but she had discovered that it was easier to do that if she stayed busy.

"I'm glad to hear it," Clay said. "Why don't you take a break?"

She sighed. "I'd rather keep busy."

"I think you might want to check out the next contestant in the steer-roping competition," Clay said. "A certain city slicker is determined to prove he's got what it takes to be a cowboy."

"Will?"

Clay just shrugged.

"Are you crazy? He can ride. But roping a steer? That's dangerous," Amberley said.

"The man has something to prove," Clay said.

"Yeah, that he's lost his mind," Amberley said, taking off at a run toward the steer-roping ring. She pushed her way to the front of the crowd and saw Erin and Faye standing there. Erin just shook her head when Amberley walked up to her.

"Can you believe this? I always thought he was a smart guy," Erin said. "I'm afraid to watch this."

"Me, too. What is he thinking?"

"That he must prove something," Erin said. "Or

maybe he isn't. You know how guys and testosterone are."

She did. But Will had always seemed different. She leaned on the railing and looked across the way at the bay where the steer was waiting to be released and then saw Will waiting, as well.

"Will Brady!" she yelled.

He looked over to her.

"You're going to get yourself killed."

"Well, I love you, cowgirl and I need to prove that I'm worthy to be your man. So if I die at least I'll die happy."

What?

He loved her.

She didn't have a chance to respond as the steer was released and Will went into action. He roped the steer on his second try and in a few seconds he had it subdued. He'd had a good teacher and she suspected it had been Clay Everett. She ran around the ring to where Will was as he entered and threw herself into his arms.

He caught her.

"Did you mean it?" she asked.

"Yes. I love you."

"I love you, too."

He kissed her long and hard, and cheers and applause broke out. When he set her on her feet Erin brought Faye over to them. Will wrapped the two of them in his arms.

"Now my world is right. I have both of my girls back here in my arms."

He led them away from the crowd.

"I'm sorry I left the way I did. I was afraid of

letting you down and of not being the man you needed."

"It's okay. I kept forgetting that you were going through firsts and that I promised you time."

"I've had all the time I need."

"I'm glad."

Later that evening, after Faye had been bathed and put to bed, Will carried Amberley down the hall to the bedroom.

He put her on her feet next to the bed. "I can't believe you're really here, cowgirl."

"I can't believe you participated in a steer-roping competition for me," she said. He was everything she had always wanted in a man and never thought she'd find.

He was perfect for her.

He leaned down and kissed her so tenderly.

"Believe it, Amberley. There is nothing I won't do for you."

He undressed her slowly, caressing her skin and then following the path of his hands with his mouth. She couldn't think as he stood back up and lifted her onto the bed. He bent down to capture the tip of her breast in his mouth. He sucked her deep in his mouth, his teeth lightly scraping against her sensitive flesh. His other hand played at her other breast, arousing her, making her arch against him in need.

She reached between them and took his erection in her hand, bringing him closer to her. She spread her legs wider so that she was totally open to him. "I need you now."

He lifted his head; the tips of her breasts were

damp from his mouth and very tight. He rubbed his chest over them before sliding deep into her body.

She slid her hands down his back, cupping his butt as he thrust deeper into her. Their eyes met—staring deep into his eyes made her feel like their souls were meeting. She'd never believed in finding Mr. Right. Everything that had happened to her at eighteen had made it seem as if that wasn't in the cards for her. Everything that was until she met Will.

She felt her body start to tighten around him, catching her by surprise. She climaxed before him. He gripped her hips, holding her down and thrusting into her two more times before he came with a loud grunt of her name.

She slid her hands up his back and kissed him deeply. "You are so much wilder than that steer I tried to tame earlier."

His deep laughter washed over her and she felt like she'd found her place here in his arms. The family she'd always craved and never thought she'd have.

He held her afterward, pulling her into his arms and tucking her up against his side. She wrapped her arm around him and listened to the solid beating of his heart. She understood that Will was going to need her by his side, not because he didn't respect her need to be independent, but because of the way Lucy had been taken from him.

She understood him so much better now than she ever could have before. And because she had her own weaknesses, she didn't want him to feel that way with her. Will had given her back something she wasn't sure she could have found on her own.

"Are you sleeping?" he asked.

She felt the vibration of his words through his chest under her ear. She shifted in his embrace, tipping her head so she could see the underside of his jaw.

"No. Too much to think about." This had been at once the most terrifying and exciting day of her life. She felt like if she went to sleep she might wake up and find none of it had happened. "I'm not sure I can live in Bellevue. I mean, my life—"

"We're not going to live in Bellevue. I'm going to buy a ranch right here in Royal. Someplace where you can have as many horses as you want and we can raise Faye and maybe adopt some brothers and sisters for her."

"You'd do that?"

"Yes. Frankly, the thought of you being pregnant would have scared the crap out of me. I wouldn't have wanted to risk losing you and there are plenty of kids in the world who need parents," he said, rubbing his hand down her back. "Does a big family sound good to you?"

"It does," she said.

He rubbed his hand up and down her arm. "Perfect. So I guess you're going to have to marry me."

She propped herself up on his chest, looking down at him in the shadowy night. "Are you asking me?"

He laughed at that. "No. I'm telling you. You want to, but you might come up with a reason why we should wait and I'm not going to."

"Are you sure?"

He rolled over so that she was under him. Her legs parted and he settled against her. His arms braced on either side of her body, he caught her head in his hands and brought his mouth down hard on hers. When he came up for air, long minutes later, he said, "I promise I most definitely am."

She believed him. Will wasn't the kind of man to make promises lightly. When he gave his word, he kept it.

"Will?"

"Right here," he said, sinking back down next to her on the bed.

"I love you, city slicker."

"And I love you, cowgirl."

* * * * *

TAKING HOME THE TYCOON
by USA TODAY bestselling author
Catherine Mann
BILLIONAIRE'S BABY BIND
by USA TODAY bestselling author
Katherine Garbera

and

November 2017:
THE TEXAN TAKES A WIFE
by USA TODAY bestselling author
Charlene Sands

December 2017:
BEST MAN UNDER THE MISTLETOE
by Jules Bennett

***

If you're on Twitter, tell us what you think of
Harlequin Desire! #harlequindesire

MILLS & BOON®
Hardback – October 2017

ROMANCE

Claimed for the Leonelli Legacy	Lynne Graham
The Italian's Pregnant Prisoner	Maisey Yates
Buying His Bride of Convenience	Michelle Smart
The Tycoon's Marriage Deal	Melanie Milburne
Undone by the Billionaire Duke	Caitlin Crews
His Majesty's Temporary Bride	Annie West
Bound by the Millionaire's Ring	Dani Collins
The Virgin's Shock Baby	Heidi Rice
Whisked Away by Her Sicilian Boss	Rebecca Winters
The Sheikh's Pregnant Bride	Jessica Gilmore
A Proposal from the Italian Count	Lucy Gordon
Claiming His Secret Royal Heir	Nina Milne
Sleigh Ride with the Single Dad	Alison Roberts
A Firefighter in Her Stocking	Janice Lynn
A Christmas Miracle	Amy Andrews
Reunited with Her Surgeon Prince	Marion Lennox
Falling for Her Fake Fiancé	Sue MacKay
The Family She's Longed For	Lucy Clark
Billionaire Boss, Holiday Baby	Janice Maynard
Billionaire's Baby Bind	Katherine Garbera

MILLS & BOON®
Large Print – October 2017

ROMANCE

Sold for the Greek's Heir	Lynne Graham
The Prince's Captive Virgin	Maisey Yates
The Secret Sanchez Heir	Cathy Williams
The Prince's Nine-Month Scandal	Caitlin Crews
Her Sinful Secret	Jane Porter
The Drakon Baby Bargain	Tara Pammi
Xenakis's Convenient Bride	Dani Collins
Her Pregnancy Bombshell	Liz Fielding
Married for His Secret Heir	Jennifer Faye
Behind the Billionaire's Guarded Heart	Leah Ashton
A Marriage Worth Saving	Therese Beharrie

HISTORICAL

The Debutante's Daring Proposal	Annie Burrows
The Convenient Felstone Marriage	Jenni Fletcher
An Unexpected Countess	Laurie Benson
Claiming His Highland Bride	Terri Brisbin
Marrying the Rebellious Miss	Bronwyn Scott

MEDICAL

Their One Night Baby	Carol Marinelli
Forbidden to the Playboy Surgeon	Fiona Lowe
A Mother to Make a Family	Emily Forbes
The Nurse's Baby Secret	Janice Lynn
The Boss Who Stole Her Heart	Jennifer Taylor
Reunited by Their Pregnancy Surprise	Louisa Heaton

MILLS & BOON®
Hardback – November 2017

ROMANCE

The Italian's Christmas Secret	Sharon Kendrick
A Diamond for the Sheikh's Mistress	Abby Green
The Sultan Demands His Heir	Maya Blake
Claiming His Scandalous Love-Child	Julia James
Valdez's Bartered Bride	Rachael Thomas
The Greek's Forbidden Princess	Annie West
Kidnapped for the Tycoon's Baby	Louise Fuller
A Night, A Consequence, A Vow	Angela Bissell
Christmas with Her Millionaire Boss	Barbara Wallace
Snowbound with an Heiress	Jennifer Faye
Newborn Under the Christmas Tree	Sophie Pembroke
His Mistletoe Proposal	Christy McKellen
The Spanish Duke's Holiday Proposal	Robin Gianna
The Rescue Doc's Christmas Miracle	Amalie Berlin
Christmas with Her Daredevil Doc	Kate Hardy
Their Pregnancy Gift	Kate Hardy
A Family Made at Christmas	Scarlet Wilson
Their Mistletoe Baby	Karin Baine
The Texan Takes a Wife	Charlene Sands
Twins for the Billionaire	Sarah M. Anderson

MILLS & BOON®
Large Print – November 2017

ROMANCE

The Pregnant Kavakos Bride	Sharon Kendrick
The Billionaire's Secret Princess	Caitlin Crews
Sicilian's Baby of Shame	Carol Marinelli
The Secret Kept from the Greek	Susan Stephens
A Ring to Secure His Crown	Kim Lawrence
Wedding Night with Her Enemy	Melanie Milburne
Salazar's One-Night Heir	Jennifer Hayward
The Mysterious Italian Houseguest	Scarlet Wilson
Bound to Her Greek Billionaire	Rebecca Winters
Their Baby Surprise	Katrina Cudmore
The Marriage of Inconvenience	Nina Singh

HISTORICAL

Ruined by the Reckless Viscount	Sophia James
Cinderella and the Duke	Janice Preston
A Warriner to Rescue Her	Virginia Heath
Forbidden Night with the Warrior	Michelle Willingham
The Foundling Bride	Helen Dickson

MEDICAL

Mummy, Nurse...Duchess?	Kate Hardy
Falling for the Foster Mum	Karin Baine
The Doctor and the Princess	Scarlet Wilson
Miracle for the Neurosurgeon	Lynne Marshall
English Rose for the Sicilian Doc	Annie Claydon
Engaged to the Doctor Sheikh	Meredith Webber

MILLS & BOON®

Why shop at millsandboon.co.uk?

Each year, thousands of romance readers find their perfect read at millsandboon.co.uk. That's because we're passionate about bringing you the very best romantic fiction. Here are some of the advantages of shopping at www.millsandboon.co.uk:

* **Get new books first**—you'll be able to buy your favourite books one month before they hit the shops

* **Get exclusive discounts**—you'll also be able to buy our specially created monthly collections, with up to 50% off the RRP

* **Find your favourite authors**—latest news, interviews and new releases for all your favourite authors and series on our website, plus ideas for what to try next

* **Join in**—once you've bought your favourite books, don't forget to register with us to rate, review and join in the discussions

Visit **www.millsandboon.co.uk**
for all this and more today!